THE BOY
NEXT DOOR

candY APPLe books...
Just for you.
sweet. Fresh. Fun.
take a bite!

THE BOY NEXT DOOR

by LAURA DOWER

CANDY APPLE

SCHOLASTIC INC.

New York Toronto London Auckland Sydney
Mexico City New Delhi Hong Kong Buenos Aires

No part of this publication may be reproduced, stored in a retrieval system, or transmitted in any form or by any means, electronic, mechanical, photocopying, recording, or otherwise, without written permission of the publisher. For information regarding permission, write to Scholastic Inc., Attention: Permissions Department, 557 Broadway, New York, NY 10012.

ISBN-13: 978-0-439-89057-1
ISBN-10: 0-439-89057-8

12 11 10 9 8 7 6 5 4 3   7 8 9 10 11/0
Printed in the U.S.A.   40
First Scholastic Printing, October 2006

For Myles and Livi

TABLE OF CONTENTS

Chapter 1

❀❀❀ TARYN ❀❀❀

I Guess It's a Boy Thing

"Jeff Rasmussen, I'm going to get you for this!" I scream at the top of my lungs.

My head pounds and I reach up to make sure there's no bump. Meanwhile, Jeff zips across my lawn into his own backyard, taunting me the whole time.

"You can run," I scream even louder, "but you can't hide!"

I can't believe Jeff would do this. Sure, he's been teasing me for eleven summers straight. There have been times over the years when he's even dared to pinch or poke me, but he usually keeps his distance. And he never actually *hit* me with

1

anything before, especially not a flying object. Mostly he just calls me obnoxious names like "stinky" and "bones. " He sure knows how to make me squirm, the rat.

Of course, I've plotted my own kind of revenge. It drives Jeff crazy when I tease him right back about the two extra-long toes on his left foot. And I got him once with a mean triple-knuckled noogie. The main difference between my teasing and his, however, are the aftershocks.

A single harsh word from Jeff and I'm bawling for five minutes.

But Jeff's different. He never ever cries. He just laughs out loud.

I guess it's a boy thing.

Jeff's family and my family have been friends forever. His mom and my mom always remind us that Jeff and I were born on the exact same week-end at the same hospital in Rochester, New York. We both weighed exactly seven pounds and four ounces, and measured twenty inches. Sometimes I wonder if Jeff is actually my secret twin brother, except that I don't really need (or want) another brother. I already have three of those: Tim, Tom, and Todd. Three Taylor brothers is more than enough for anyone.

I guess the worst part about Jeff's sneak attack

today was that he didn't hit me with a Wiffle ball or anything accidental. No, he hit me with a sneaker aimed directly at my head — a smelly, brown, disgusting sneaker with a rubber sole that's peeling off.

How gross is that?

"Jeff, where are you?" I growl, climbing over the break in the fence between our houses. I scramble through the thicket, trying hard not to scratch up my legs. I'm already covered from head to toe with mosquito bites.

It's too warm out today. The air feels like mashed potatoes and I can't find Jeff anywhere. He's not in the small shed behind his house. He's not under his front porch. I've checked all of his usual hiding spots.

I'm getting thirsty.

"Jeff, come out!" I cry. "Come on, it's too hot. Truce? Please?"

Jeff appears from around the side of his blue-shingled house. He's whistling and carrying two Popsicles. I take a cherry one. He keeps the lime. We sit on the porch steps. I realize that he's still only wearing one sneaker, the one he didn't hurl at my head.

"That really, really hurt, you know," I grumble, biting the end of my Popsicle.

He looks right through me. "Yeah, sorry, Taryn," he says. I want to believe him, but he's smirking.

"You're sorry?" I repeat, my eyes widening.

"Yeah, sorry. Truly."

"You mean it?" I ask, twisting the ends of my long, brown hair.

"Yeah," Jeff replies. "I didn't really mean to hit you. I just got carried away. And I know how gross my sneakers are."

He sounds genuine this time. As if.

But somehow, despite all the teasing over the years, Jeff always finds the right thing to say or do to make things better. Somehow, a word or even just a smile is like a Band-Aid, and I can instantly forgive Jeff for whatever he's done.

That's how it works with best friends.

Jeff leaves me on the porch with his Popsicle peace offering and races across the lawn, back to my yard. He's gone to find his other stinky shoe. He returns with both sneakers laced up and a yellow dandelion tight in his fist.

"Here," Jeff grunts, pushing the little flower toward me.

Now it's my turn to laugh. "Thanks," I say with a smile, taking the flower. It's peace offering number two. I'm secretly glad that he's feeling so guilty.

The sun beats down hard on the steps, so we

move up to the wicker rocking chairs on his porch. We've spent more afternoons than I can count rocking in those chairs together. Sometimes we play Scrabble or cards out there. Sometimes his mom makes us peanut-butter-and-marshmallow sandwiches. Sometimes his Maltese, Toots, sits on my lap, while my cat, Zsa-Zsa, sits on his lap. We tickle their ears and sing dumb songs.

Today, all we can think or talk about is sixth grade. It's already late August and school is right around the corner. We're moving to Westcott Middle School from the elementary school down the street. That means that I'll be taking a bus to school every morning instead of walking with Jeff.

Mom got a letter from school the other day that listed the different sixth-grade homerooms. I'm in 10A. Jeff is in 11B. I hate the fact that Jeff and I won't be in the same room. It will be the first time in all of our years in school together that we'll start each day in a different class with a different teacher. My best girlfriends, Leslie and Cristina, are in my homeroom, so I guess I'll survive.

But it won't be the same.

"Westcott has an awesome soccer team," Jeff mumbles, taking a final lick of his drippy Popsicle.

"Yeah, everyone knows that," I say.

Jeff likes soccer more than almost anything

else — even more than Toots. And that's saying something. He's been dreaming about winning a World Cup title since he was little. Fifth-grade soccer camp, and fourth-grade camp before that, just didn't cut the mustard. He has at least three pairs of cleats in his closet. Late this summer, Jeff was a part of this youth soccer league in our town. The kids told him that even though he was going into sixth grade, sometimes really good players were allowed to join the seventh and eighth grade middle school team. Now that's all he can talk about. He wants to be the exception to the rule.

"What are *you* going to do at Westcott?" Jeff asks with the usual daydream-y look in his eye that he always gets when thinking about soccer.

"What do you mean? Like after school?"

Jeff nods. "Yeah."

"I haven't really thought about it. I guess I'll try out for the school play, or maybe the school paper," I reply, licking my sticky, cherry fingers.

"Yeah," Jeff grunts. "You would."

"What is that supposed to mean?"

"*Nada.*"

I stand up and readjust my shorts, leaning back just a little so the sun isn't in my eyes. "Don't be a toad," I caution him, wagging my index finger in his face.

Jeff laughs and pinches me on the arm.

"Ribbit," he croaks, dancing off the porch steps.

Ow! I can almost feel the imaginary steam escaping out of my ears as I chase him around a tree, circle his shed, and speed back up the porch steps.

"Tag, you're it!" I shout, leaning in for the touch. But just as I brush his arm, I catch my toe on a step and go flying.

Splat.

Jeff gets this stunned look for a split second. Then he bursts into a fit of hyena laughter. Here I am, sprawled on the steps, and he doesn't even try to help me up.

Instead, he *tags* me.

"You're it again!" Jeff hollers.

Just then, two boys appear at the fence gate near the side of Jeff's house. It's Jeff's best guy friends, Peter and Anthony. They're starting sixth grade at Westcott in a few weeks, too.

"Hey, Taryn, nice fall," Peter calls out to me.

I want to laugh, but my knee is killing me.

Jeff shoots me an abrupt look that says, "Okay, see you later. I have to hang out with the guys now." He's been giving me that look all summer long. We used to hang out together, the four of us, but lately they don't seem to want a girl around. I'm not sure why.

I wish I could pull off my own shoe and hit Jeff on the head with it, right there in front of his friends, so he would know how it feels. But somehow I don't think a flimsy pink flip-flop will have quite the same effect as his smelly sneaker. And I don't really want to hurt anyone, especially not him.

So I slink away from the boys, taking the hint, waving and hiking back through the break in Jeff's just-painted gray fence. In a few minutes, I'm back in my own yard, sidestepping my mother's purple daisies.

My brother Tim is lying in a lawn chair with his sunglasses on. He's as ginger-brown as an almond. He's spent the whole summer perfecting his tan. His girlfriend, Amy, works at a tanning parlor. The two of them look like an unnatural color to me, but I'm no tanning expert.

"Yo, Taryn, you got a phone call," Tim calls out to me.

"From who?" I ask.

"Dr. Wexler," Tim says, giving me a dramatic, low whistle and peering over the tops of his dark shades. "He wanted to schedule your eye exam. Man, are you in trouble, sis. That guy's Dr. Dread if you ask me."

"Ha, ha, ha . . . No one asked you," I groan, rolling my eyes and trying to act cool. I skip up the steps up to our house and push open the screen door.

The last person in the world I want to think about right now is Dr. Wexler.

Ever since I found out that I my eyes don't work right, Tim's been trying to scare me about the optometrist. I hate to admit it, but his big-brother tactics are beginning to work. I'm trying hard not to be scared about the whole experience, but how am I supposed to feel about wearing glasses for the rest of my life? I know Tim's right about Dr. Wexler, too. Everyone says that guy has cold hands and death breath when he leans in to check your vision.

It all started at school last year, when I couldn't see the board. I didn't say anything at first, but then my grades started to slip. Then I found myself getting eye aches and sitting really close to the TV. And then I failed that stupid eye test the nurse gave me. The only reason I'm getting glasses at all is because Mom and Dad didn't give me a choice. Otherwise, I'd be perfectly content to walk around in a blurry haze for the rest of my life.

When I wander into the kitchen, I'm not surprised to find Mom there, chopping carrots.

"Are you in or out?" she asks me. "I'm trying a new recipe and I need all the taste buds I can find."

Mom's always experimenting in the kitchen. I think she dreams of being on Iron Chef one day, making weird dishes with rutabaga and octopus. I prefer grilled cheese myself.

"I'm in," I say, and take a seat at the table. My other brothers are, of course, nowhere to be found. "What's on the menu today, Mom?"

Her face lights up and she pushes some kind of salad in front of me. It smells like vinegar and onions. Cautiously, I lift a forkful into my mouth.

"So? So?" Mom hops up and down in front of me, looking for some kind of reaction.

Of course, I know what to say.

"Deeeee-licious," I mumble, choking down the salad. Mom beams.

Dad says Mom's sick of predictable dinners, so she's always looking for new recipes to try. And all summer I've been trying, really trying to deal. But it's hard.

And it's not just about the food.

School starts in exactly two weeks and I want to know one thing: Isn't there some way to make sure that, in sixth grade, things can just stay the way they've always been?

Chapter 2

• • • Jeff • • •

Call Me Worm King

"I dare you to eat one of those," Peter says, pointing to a brown, crusty leaf on a burned-out bush.

"No prob," I say, grabbing the dead leaf and shoving it into my mouth. It crunches loudly as my friends laugh.

We're always playing games like this. Peter and my other buddy Anthony are pretty good with doing certain dares. They'll walk on rickety fences, climb jagged rocks, and jump into cold lakes. But they won't eat half the stuff I will. This summer alone, I've swallowed a ladybug, twelve pebbles, a dish of dirt, and a long list of other things, including half of a moldy cheese sandwich. They wouldn't even take a single bite.

"Okay," Anthony pipes up after I've swallowed the leaf. "Now you need to . . ."

"Wait a minute," I interrupt him. "It's *your* turn."

Anthony makes a face. "All right," he says begrudgingly. "Bring it on."

Peter has an idea right away. He's spotted something in the grass. He leans down and holds it up. It's a fat, wet earthworm.

"Gross me out," Anthony says, tightening his lips. "You want me to eat that? Uhh, no way, man."

I cluck like a chicken.

"If you're so brave, you do it," Anthony says, glaring at Peter.

Peter looks momentarily stunned by the reverse dare.

"I-I-" Peter stammers. "I don't think so."

I step in and reach for the worm. It's cold.

"You guys are wimps," I declare, throwing the wriggling thing into my mouth and taking one quick gulp.

The only thing is: I don't really eat the worm. I toss it over my shoulder. It's a trick I've been practicing for years. But Peter and Anthony don't see.

Suckers.

"No way!" Anthony screams.

"You didn't!" Peter joins in.

"It's so salty," I say, gagging and pretending to chomp on the worm. "Mmmm. Mud and guts . . ."

By now my friends are both frowning *and* cracking up at the same time.

"That's just way too gross, dude," Anthony says, making a face. "I can't believe you —"

"Hold on!" Peter screams. "What's that?"

He points to my shoulder. *Oops.* The worm never made it into the grass at all. Now it's inching toward my neck.

"You faked us out?" Anthony says, slapping me on my arm.

My cheeks get hot. I shrug.

"Excellent!" Peter says, giving me a high five in appreciation of my prank.

I fling the worm off my shoulder, and the three of us double over with laughter. As far as they're concerned, I'm the funniest thing they've ever seen. A sense of pride takes over.

"You might as well just crown me now," I announce. "From now on you can call me Worm King."

That only makes Anthony laugh harder.

We quit the dares and play a few innings of Wiffle ball until Peter grand slams the ball over our neighbor's fence. Then the guys get on their bikes and head home. I head for our porch steps.

I lean back, feet crossed in front, counting a trail of bruises from my ankle to my knee. As clouds drift by, the sun begins to dip down until I can't see it anymore. It won't be dark for an hour or more, but the sky fades from blue to white to pink. Leaves rustle.

I can't wait to call Taryn and tell her about the great worm fake out. The last time I ate anything that crawled, she practically threw up. She loves my bug stories. I can tell.

Maybe I should have asked her over to play Xbox with me tonight. I thought about it, but then she seemed annoyed at me about the sneaker incident. I still have no idea why I threw my shoe at her head. It seemed so funny at the time.

"Jeffrey!" Mom shouts from behind the screen door. "Get inside, will you?"

My stomach does a massive roller-coaster flop. I feel like Mom's been on my case in a major way all summer long.

In June she made me cut my hair really short. I looked like I'd been attacked by a lawn mower.

In July, she started ironing my T-shirts. All she talked about was all the wrinkles in my clothes.

This month, for some reason, she's freaking out about sixth grade. Since I nearly flunked fifth-grade math, Mom wants to make sure that I take math more seriously this year. I tried explaining to her that I *do* take school seriously, and she bought it; at least for a little while. Then she made me this killer deal. In middle school, if I get a B or higher in math, she'll buy me tickets to a pro baseball or hockey game.

I can't blow that bargain.

"Coming!" I scream at the top of my lungs, even though Mom's only a few yards away.

As I leap up and fling open the screen door, Mom's standing there with her hands wrapped in a tight knot at her waist.

"Is it really necessary to yell?" Mom asks, smirking.

"You always tell me to speak up for myself."

"Jeffrey . . ."

"Sorry," I say.

Mom grabs my earlobe and smiles. "You're a beast," she teases, pretending to yank me inside. She's not pulling very hard, but I yelp in fake pain. Then she hugs me. It's just this thing we do.

"I need to get supper in the oven. Your step-father has to stay late at work again," Mom explains as we stroll into the kitchen together. She picks up a handful of untrimmed green beans from a bowl on the table.

"Care to snip?" she asks.

I take a pair of scissors from the drawer and park myself in front of the bowl.

Rowwwf!

My half sister, Blair, races into the kitchen chasing our dog, Toots. The dog is wearing a pink doll's dress with two snaps shut, a polka-dotted bow looped around his collar, and these teeny purple glitter barrettes by his ears. As he scampers up into my lap, his little pink tongue flaps. In no time, my shirt is covered in drool.

"What's wrong with Toots?" Blair whines. "He won't sit still. And I haven't finished fixing his fur."

Blair whines all the time, especially when she doesn't get her way. She's only eight, but she has something to say about everything.

"Nothing is wrong with Toots," I snap at my sister. "And in case you hadn't noticed, he's a *boy* dog. . . ."

"Jeffrey," Mom says in a stern voice, cutting me right off. She knows I am about to say that the problem is not Toots, but Blair. But Mom also knows that if I say this, Blair will throw one of her princess fits.

"Jeffy, give me back the doggy," Blair demands.

Groaning, I kiss the top of Toots's head and place him gently onto the floor. "Good luck, buddy," I whisper.

16

Toots takes off for the living room. Blair zooms after him.

Five minutes later, the bowl of beans is perfectly snipped. I dump them into our microwavable steamer and ask Mom what else she needs. She kisses me on my head and says, "Nothing." That's exactly what I hoped she'd say.

It's still warm and the sky is light, so I head back out to the porch again, plopping into one of the wicker rockers. From where I sit, I can see up into the windows of Taryn's house. She's walking around . . . now she's petting Zsa-Zsa . . . no, she's reading a book.

Ever since we were kids, Taryn and I have played spies, inventing secret ways to communicate between our two houses. We hold up notes in our windows with short messages, sometimes even coded ones. Other times we try to disguise our voices on the telephone. One time, we tried to string a couple of cans across the yard from window to window, like old-fashioned walkie-talkies.

It was a great experiment until the wind blew. That's when the string wrapped itself around a row of cables. My stepdad, J.D., still busts on me for that one. I don't know how it happened, but that lousy string knocked out our cable TV for two days, just before one of his big football games.

And J.D.'s like an elephant. He never forgets.

The screen door to the front porch opens with a loud squeak.

"Jeffy, Mom wants you again," Blair says.

I ignore her, as usual.

"Jeffy, Mom wants you NOW," Blair says again, louder this time.

I keep looking the other way.

"Move your butt, bro!"

"Watch your mouth, sis," I shoot back, knowing that if Mom hears Blair talking like that, the only person who will get into trouble is me.

I amble inside to find out what Mom wants now. It's a phone call for me. She stands there, arm extended with the portable. I can hear breathing on the other end.

"Guess who?" Mom asks.

I know who. I take the phone.

"Hey, Taryn," I say into the receiver.

"How did you know it was me?" Taryn asks. Her voice sounds muffled.

"Where are you?" I ask. "It sounds like you're in a tunnel." I wonder if she's pulling one of our old secret agent tricks.

"Duh, I'm in my room," Taryn says matter-of-factly. "But you know that already, don't you? I saw you on the porch, Jeff."

"You saw me?" I can't help but laugh out loud. "Spying, right?"

Taryn laughs right back. "Hey, are you guys having dinner soon?" she asks.

"Nah. Sounds like J.D.'s going to be late again. What about you?"

"Mom's cooking. Want to meet up later for flashlight tag?" Taryn asks. "Maybe Peter and Anthony can come over, too? I think that kid Mike from down the street is back from camp. Your sister could even play."

"My sister? You're kidding, right?" I grunt.

"Whatever. Just meet me when it gets dark," Taryn says.

"Okay," I say. I'll do almost anything for a good game of flashlight tag. So far this summer I'm undefeated in our neighborhood. Not that anyone really keeps score except for me.

"Meet you by the shed," Taryn says.

As I hang up the phone, I wonder just how many good games of flashlight tag we'll play for the rest of August and then September.

I miss summer already.

Chapter 3

❀ ❀ ❀ TARYN ❀ ❀ ❀

A Very Big Biggie

It was all Cristina's idea in fourth grade. She decided to take the letters of each of our first names and make up a new name for the three of us. And so we became TLC, for Taryn, Leslie, and Cristina, otherwise known as Tender Loving Care.

I admit it was kind of dumb, calling ourselves something like the name of an old singing group, but after a short time the name grew on me. And then it just stuck like Elmer's.

Today, I'm hanging with L and C down at the town pool. I wish this weather lasted all year long. I hate knowing that summer has to end. Sometimes I fantasize that we live in Hawaii and not New York. Then we'd have our own surf club.

We'd know how to do the hula. I'm sure my brother Tim wouldn't mind being tanned and eating pineapple all year long.

The only yucky thing this summer was my bathing suit. I've been wearing the same-style one-piece, tank suit forever. This summer L and C got these cute new flower bikinis with little ties on the side. Leslie's hair got really blond so she looks like a swimsuit model. Cristina started wearing makeup, even when it's ninety degrees or hotter.

I wonder if anyone notices this stuff besides me.

Next year it's definitely my turn to get a bikini.

Bathing suits aside, swimming at the town pool is just the best. The pool has three different diving levels, and this summer I finally made the monster leap off the high board. There is no better feeling than jumping off a diving board into cold water when it's scorching hot out. Even a belly flop feels okay as long as it cools me off.

The three of us have spent a lot of time together at the pool for the past few summers, but this summer was by far the busiest — and the most interesting. Leslie declared a mega-crush on a lifeguard named Rick, and he's in ninth grade. He's so old, he has facial hair. I don't get it. What's the big deal about this guy?

Cristina's cousin came up from Puerto Rico for

a few weeks, too. She was super-duper nice and her name was Ellen, so Cristina briefly changed our name from TLC to TLCE, or, Tender Loving Care Etcetera. Cristina is always so good with words. She's won the school spelling bee three years in a row.

Now it's the last week before sixth grade, and I haven't seen much of Jeff around the pool lately. He's busy with a math tutor or something. He won't say. I think he's embarrassed. His mother is worried about school already, not that it's any big surprise. She worries about everything. I am so glad my mom's not a worrywart, bugging me about grades and report cards before school even starts.

"So did you decide on your first-day outfit?" Leslie asks Cristina and me.

Cristina breaks into a wide smile. "Of course!" she chirps. "Black pants and tank top. Perfect."

"Black?" Leslie moans.

"What's wrong with black? It's in all the magazines," Cristina says.

"Black isn't even a real color," Leslie gripes. "We should give you a makeover."

Cristina lets out one of her little snort-laughs. "Yeah, right!" she says.

Leslie laughs right back. "It could be fun. . . ." she says in a singsongy voice. "Remember when we dyed your hair with blue Kool-Aid on your birthday last year?"

"Yeah, and I remember my mom having a fit when the color didn't wash out for a month," Cristina says.

"What are you wearing, Leslie?" I ask. I'm always tempted still — after all these years — to call her Les, but I know she'd hate me for that. Leslie doesn't believe in nicknames anymore.

"I got this incredible new shirt and these turquoise Capri pants that fit me perfectly," Leslie says. "Plus, I'm getting my hair cut the day before school starts."

"What about you, Taryn?" Cristina asks me.

I say something incomprehensible about jeans and a T-shirt. The truth is, I don't have a clue about what to wear on the first day of sixth grade. I hadn't really thought about it before now. Jeff and I never talk about things like outfits. He wears the same kind of clothes every day.

"Oh, look. Check *her* out," Leslie says, nudging me and Cristina.

She's staring at Emma Wallace, one of our classmates and my neighbor. As usual, Emma's decked out in a perfect watermelon-pink two piece bathing suit. She's even wearing matching pink sunglasses. Everything complements her shoulder-length, chestnut brown curls, long legs, and white teeth. She has these pouty lips like movie stars have — but hers are the real deal. And I'm pretty sure she's never, ever had a pimple.

Worst of all, she's nice.

"Does she think she's a supermodel or what?" Cristina groans.

I have to giggle. Sometimes I feel like Zsa-Zsa, claws out, when we're talking about other people this way. I wonder what people say about me when I'm not around.

"Forget Miss Perfect. Look who's over *there*," Cristina whispers, indicating the deep end of the pool. "It's Danny Bogart. I haven't seen him all summer. He's grown, like, ten inches taller. Wow."

"He is cute, isn't he?" Leslie giggles.

"You both think everyone is cute," I say.

I stare off to catch a glimpse of Danny for myself. He's playing Marco Polo with a bunch of other guys we know from elementary school. It looks like all of them went through summer growth spurts. I hadn't noticed until now.

"I wish someone would ask me out on a date," Cristina declares.

I look at her like she has six heads. "What?" Mom has already told me I can't date until high school, so I don't even think about it.

"Now that we're in sixth grade," Cristina continues, "we all need to find someone to like."

"What are you guys talking about?" I ask.

"I already like someone." Leslie giggles, covering her face with her hands. Her cheeks look more sunburned than usual when she says that.

"Who?" I ask, surprised. She hasn't said anything about this before now.

Leslie moves her hands away long enough to mumble, "Charlie."

Right away, Cristina and I know she means Charlie West, this guy from last year's homeroom. He and Jeff play basketball sometimes.

"Charlie?" I say, rolling my eyes. "Why him?"

Leslie giggles some more, which gets Cristina giggling, too. I don't get it.

"Isn't there someone that *you* like, Taryn?" Leslie asks.

"No," I say matter-of-factly.

"I think you should go out with Jeff," Cristina declares.

My eyes bug out wide. "Jeff?" I cough. "Have you totally lost your mind?"

"Why not? He's nice," Leslie says. "And he's way cuter this year than he was last year."

"Wait. You've always told me he was a dork," I say, confused.

"Nah. He just acts that way sometimes," Cristina says.

"But all boys do," Leslie adds.

This whole conversation freaks me out. "I do not like Jeff or any boy that way," I say in a firm voice.

This sends L and C into convulsive laughter. They don't believe me, no matter how many times I deny it. It's time to change the subject — fast.

Lucky for me, the conversation is cut off because Rick comes over and tells us to move. The pool is getting ready to shut down for the afternoon. There's a camp swim meet today, so free swim is over. Briefly, the three of us consider staying up in the bleachers to cheer on some of our other friends from school. But in the end, we all pick up our stuff and head to the locker room to change back into our regular clothes.

In the locker room, no one talks about boys anymore and I am totally relieved. I walk outside with Leslie and Cristina. They're getting a ride home together with Leslie's dad. After they leave, I wait on the curb for my brother Todd to show up. He just got his driver's license last year so Mom always sends him out on errands, which include picking me up.

On the way home, Todd doesn't say very much.

He's chomping on a piece of gum and listening to one of his heavy metal CDs. Ugh.

When we get inside the house, I climb up the stairs to my bedroom and grab the portable phone. Naturally, Tom's on the other line with his friends. They always play around with the three-way-calling feature. They can stay on the phone for hours, literally. It drives Mom batty. It drives me battier.

Outside my window, our giant willow tree is dancing. I see its branches sway back and forth even though the air outside was so still and hot earlier today. I wonder when autumn will show up for real. The weather forecaster said we're supposed to have another heat wave before the season changes.

Across the yard, I can see right into Jeff's bedroom window. He's there, sitting on his bed with his Game Boy. Toots is there, too, wagging his tail. I think about what Cristina and Leslie said, about Jeff being cuter this year.

He doesn't look any different to me.

I check the phone again. Tom is finally off the line so I dial Jeff's house. His little sister, Blair, answers. I'm still looking out my window into his room when I see Blair walk in carrying the phone. She hands it to him.

"Hello?" Jeff asks in a deep voice.

"Hey," I answer.

His head bobs up, and he shoots a look right out his window. Now we're on the phone, talking, but we can see each other, too.

"Missed you at the pool today," I say.

I see Jeff shrug. "I had to help J.D. clean the garage. Man, it stunk."

"Are you listening to that Lame Brain CD right now?" I ask.

Jeff nods. "Want to listen? This band totally rocks."

I nod right back, knowing he can see me, and give him a dramatic thumbs-up. He races over to his stereo to turn up the music. It blares into the phone. I wonder if it's making his windows rattle.

When we were smaller, we used to play this DJ game together. I'd be in my room, playing the announcer, and Jeff would be in his room, spinning music like a real radio disc jockey.

The Lame Brain guitarist lets his instrument wail and then the song is done. I stand right up at the window and start clapping. I can see Jeff laugh as he picks up his phone.

"So who else was at the pool?" Jeff asks.

"L and C," I say.

"Any other kids from school?"

"Jacob, Danny, Miles, Emma . . ."

I list off the names of a few other kids and that gets us blabbing about sixth grade all over again. I let it slip (again) that I'm worried about the first day of school. It's only three days away now.

"Quit obsessing, Taryn," Jeff says.

"I don't obsess," I say.

"Yes, you do," Jeff counters.

"No, I don't."

"Yes, you do."

I let out a huge sigh. "Well, I think it's perfectly normal to worry."

"Whatever."

"Hey, can we take the bus together on the first day?"

"Of course," Jeff says matter-of-factly. "What else were we going to do?"

"I don't know," I reply, feeling silly for asking the question.

"Sixth grade will be no biggie, Taryn. Trust me." Now Jeff sounds a little annoyed.

I really want to believe my best friend. I want to believe that getting used to a new school and new teachers will be a piece of chocolate cake. But something tells me that Jeff is way wrong. Something tells me that sixth grade at Westcott is going to be a *very big* biggie.

And I still have no idea what I'm going to wear.

Chapter 4

• • • Jeff • • •

The Bus Stops Here

Here comes Mom again. She's got that red-in-the-face expression, even though she's smiling at the same time.

"Jeffrey, dear, why is everything from your closet now on the floor?" she asks, still smiling.

"Um . . . er . . ."

I don't know what to say. Even worse, I don't know what to wear for the first day of sixth grade.

"Do we have a fashion emergency?" Mom jokes.

"Naw," I bark defensively. "I've got everything under control. *Everything*."

Quickly, I grab the first pair of pants and polo shirt I see. The pants are corduroy and I can't remember the last time they were washed. The

30

shirt is clean (I think), but it's been in a ball in the back of my closet for as long as I can remember. It's a little bit — okay, *a lot* — wrinkled.

"Oh, Jeffrey, take those off!" Mom wails, sounding mad. "Those are winter pants."

Mom makes me exchange the cords for a freshly washed pair of Levis. Then she takes the shirt from me and disappears into the next room. I push and shove the remainder of the scattered clothing into one large pile and nudge it toward my closet. This is my patented "pile" technique. I've been cleaning my room this way for years.

Half an hour later, I'm dressed, cool, and wrinkle-free (thanks to Mom), and headed next door to Taryn's. Ever since I was little, Taryn and I have walked to school together. Elementary school was a breeze. It was right up the street.

But this year it's different.

This year we have to walk three blocks to catch a bus and then head all the way across town. Our new middle school is across the railroad tracks, down by this multi-level shopping area in town. We couldn't walk there even if we wanted to.

On my way out of the house, I catch my reflection in the hall mirror. I look like J.D., all starched and pressed. Too bad there's no time to change out of this geeky shirt into a t-shirt. At least Mom got me a new backpack with my initials on the pocket. That adds some cool to the outfit.

Just as I'm leaving, my half sister, Blair, appears. She's wearing this yellow-striped dress I hate with these brown Mary Jane shoes I hate even more. Even worse, this morning she's actually skipping around the house and singing way off-key. Peter, Anthony, and I always joke that she was cloned from a bad episode of Barney the dinosaur.

"Shake a leg, Jeffrey," Mom says. "Taryn's on her front steps. She's waiting. I can see her from here. You have everything? Did you put your soccer cleats in your bag? I know you said you might —"

"Got 'em," I say impatiently, grabbing the new backpack.

"You look very handsome, dear," Mom says, brushing something off my shoulder. Mom is always plucking some kind of imaginary lint off my clothes.

"Mom," I groan. "Good-bye. Okay?"

"Okay," she says in a soothing voice. "Have a great first day of school."

Blair yells, "Good-bye, Jeffy!" at the top of her lungs, and Mom tells me to say good-bye, but I don't. I just wave without turning around. It is bad enough that I have to tolerate a mutant half sister. I shouldn't have to give her a big good-bye, too.

Outside, the air still smells like hot dogs and

honeysuckle and everything else that's summertime to me, but I know the truth: Summer is long gone. Memories of pools and sunburns and games of flashlight tag flood my brain. Then a voice jolts me from my thoughts.

"Move it, Jeff, or we'll be late!"

It's Taryn. She waves as I jump between two bushes and jog up to her house.

"You look different," she says. Is she snickering?

"My mom made me wear this," I say. "So just shut up."

"Do you like *my* outfit?" Taryn asks me, pointing at her pink shirt and jeans.

I have no idea what to say, especially after she just insulted me.

"Yeah, sure, Taryn, it's fine," I grunt.

"Thanks," Taryn says, looking pleased by my response.

Together we head to the bus stop.

The temperature feels sauna-like, or at least what I imagine a sauna would feel like if I'd actually ever been in one. By the time we've walked two of the three blocks, I'm sweating — a lot. I really wish I was wearing a T-shirt.

"I'm nervous. Are you?" Taryn asks me.

I don't know what to say to that, either. After all, I'm the one who's sweating, right?

"I just think it's so weird, being nervous about school," Taryn says.

"Everything you think is weird," I joke.

Taryn fakes a laugh and pushes me so hard I stumble off the curb.

"Hey," I growl, jumping back onto the sidewalk.

"Sorry," Taryn says, stifling a giggle. "I guess I don't know my own strength."

"Yes, you do," I say. "You're Wonder Woman, right?"

"Very funny, Aquaman."

We both chuckle and approach the bus stop slowly. A crowd has gathered there; not just kids but mothers, fathers, and even a dalmatian, a dog that belongs to Emma Wallace. She went to elementary school with us.

"Hey, Jeff. Hey, Taryn," Emma calls out as we get closer. "How are you guys? Can you believe school is really here?"

I nod and smile but Taryn doesn't say anything. Whenever we see Emma around the neighborhood, Taryn always clams up.

"Middle school seems so . . . well . . . *major*. Doesn't it?" Emma says, smiling.

"Nah," I say.

"Nah," Taryn says, just like me. I could punch her for doing that.

I can see that Emma's dalmatian wants to jump up on me — bad. He must smell Toots all over me.

"Mom was going to drive me to school," Emma explains. "But I told her no way. I wanted to come to the bus stop so I could go to school with everyone else in our neighborhood and our class and not miss out on the whole first day of school thing, you know what I mean?"

I have no idea what she means. Still, I nod.

Taryn turns to the side and makes a face at me. Hopefully, Emma didn't catch that.

Finally, from around a corner, the yellow school bus — *our* yellow school bus — appears. A hum rises from the small crowd. The bus rolls to a stop.

"Hey, want to sit together?" Emma asks Taryn.

"That's okay," Taryn says quickly. "I'm already sitting with Jeff."

"Maybe tomorrow then," Emma says, kissing her mom and her dog good-bye and climbing up the bus steps.

Taryn and I hang back a little. I'm looking for my friends Peter and Anthony. They said they'd be here, too, but I can't see Anthony's spike haircut anywhere.

"What was *that* about?" Taryn whispers to me as soon as Emma steps away. "I had no idea she was going to ask me that."

"Yeah, weird," I mumble. I'm focused on the people ahead of us. They move like snails.

I see this seventh grader Mike who lives a few houses away from me. He has a cast on his arm and it's covered in magic marker. I wish I could read what it says. Next to him are the giraffe twins: Brittany and Bethany. They live nearby, too. I think they're starting eighth grade this year. Everyone knows them because they've been the tallest kids in our neighborhood and at school for years — taller than all the boys, even. Off to the side is Duck. His real name is Edgar, but no one ever calls him that. Duck never goes anywhere without his asthma inhaler. He got the nickname because it sounds like he quacks when he talks.

"What's the holdup?" I ask under my breath.

Taryn laughs. "Maybe it's a sign."

"Of what?"

"Maybe it's a sign that sixth grade isn't really meant to start today," Taryn says.

I roll my eyes. "Oh yeah, that's it."

Taryn's way into omens and karma and all that creepy stuff. I tried playing that Ouija game with her once, where you ask the game board a question and it "magically" spells out an answer. She thought there was some secret power guiding our fingers across the board. I half expected ghostly organ music to start playing. Get real.

When the snails move and we finally do get on the bus, I'm relieved to spot Peter and Anthony waving from the back. They must have gotten on at the last stop.

Taryn doesn't look quite as glad to see them. "I hope they saved a seat for me, too."

"Of course they did," I insist.

On our way down the bus aisle, we pass Emma and some of the other sixth graders we know from the area, plus a whole bunch of seventh and eighth graders who live nearby. Some kids grunt hello; some are too busy talking. Everyone's jabbering like crazy and the sound in the bus is so loud that I feel an instant headache coming on.

As I get closer, Peter and Anthony give me high fives. Then I sit down on the edge of the sticky, fake leather seat across from them. Meanwhile, Taryn looms right over me with this goofy look on her face.

"Move over," she commands.

I'm about to get up to let her in when the bus jerks forward. I feel myself lift up off the seat. Peter and Anthony yell out like we're on The Scream Machine.

"Wheeee!"

And then Taryn, who isn't holding on to anything, loses her footing. I reach out and grab for her backpack, but can't catch her before she hits the bus floor.

Thud.

Peter lets out a snort, then Anthony. Soon, everyone is laughing in the rows around us. Taryn tells them all to zip their lips.

It sounds like something my grandmother would say.

"Are you okay?" I lean down and whisper. I'm trying so hard not to burst out laughing myself. She's still half on the floor. Truth is, she's lucky she didn't fly out a window or slam into a seat. The bus driver glances back and asks what's up, but keeps driving. Everything's okay.

Luckily, there are no tears. Taryn gets up and pretends like nothing happened.

"That was interesting," she says, brushing off her pants.

"Break anything?" Anthony jeers, grinning.

Peter's about to say something, too, but I shoot him my insane-asylum look.

When we finally get to school, everyone's nerves are still all tingly, and not just because of Taryn's big dive. It's the realization that sixth grade is finally here — for real.

We all pile off the bus. Westcott Middle School rises up from the ground in front of us like a huge temple with columns out front. It's one of those buildings that's brand new but made to look old. The school's name is carved next to sculpted birds at the top of each column, like buildings I've seen in my history textbooks. I've been here before, once with my stepfather and once for orientation when we were still in fifth grade. But today this place looms up like some kind of monster.

That girl Emma was right. There is something so major about all of this. Sixth grade is the big-time. I should have had an extra waffle for breakfast.

As I walk toward the front doors of my new school, Taryn grabs my elbow.

"Wait up," she says.

"What?" I sigh deliberately.

"What?" Taryn repeats. Her eyebrows crinkle at the top. For the first time, I notice that the pink shirt she's wearing has a teeny black mark on the side, probably from when she fell down. I point it out.

Bad move.

In an instant, Taryn's cheeks swell out like one of those puffer fish I've seen at the aquarium.

"Taryn, you have to chill," I warn her, lying through my teeth. "The shirt looks totally fine."

"Whatever," she moans, pushing ahead of me, way ahead until she disappears in the crowd.

I let her go. I'd rather walk into school with my guy friends, anyway. Briefly, I poke my head above the crowd to see if I can spot her, but I can't see much of anything. I can't hear much of anything, either. As we move in a clump toward the school building, everyone is screaming. It's all hellos and good-byes up the steps and into the building. Then a loudspeaker blares.

"Good morning, students," the principal's voice booms. At least I think it's the principal. He sounds like somebody important.

Peter, Anthony, and I huddle together and make our way to room 11B. As we stroll inside our homeroom, a teacher with a bald head the shape of a cantaloupe hands me a stack of papers.

"Good morning," the teacher says. "Welcome to sixth grade."

I glance down at the top sheet of paper. It has a schedule grid with a bunch of strange names and subjects. How will I remember all these teacher names? How will I know where to go every day — and how to get there? How will I survive taking math and reading diagnostic tests during the first week of school? I don't even know what diagnostic means.

On the chalkboard, the teacher has written out

a short version of the day's activities. First, we have to take attendance. Then we have to fill out all these dumb forms. Then we get a tour and go to some "meet the teacher" buffet lunch. All afternoon, we'll be filling out even more forms. I'm going to need more pencils.

This seems totally unfair to me. It's the first day! Can't we have a pizza party or something? Man, this is rough. I'd much rather be tossing a ball to Toots in the backyard.

When I glance over at my friends, they look as freaked out as me about the day's activities. Peter gives me and Anthony a double thumbs-down.

I nod. It feels like the day has lasted forever — and it's only just begun.

I grab a pencil and fill in all the little boxes and lines on the page in front of me while Mr. Melon Head paces around the room. Every time I glance up at the clock on the wall, it feels like the hands haven't moved at all. Time really is standing still.

After all the first-day forms are completed, we take a break and then we get our lockers. I have locker number 235. It's so narrow. I liked my fat fifth-grade locker way better. Plus, I can't seem to memorize this new locker combination. I keep getting it mixed up with my online password numbers and my bike lock.

By the time the final bell of the school day rings, I'm spent. Melon Head lines us up to get our new textbooks and then sends us on our way. After dropping off the books in my new locker, I spot Taryn coming out of the east stairwell. She's walking with Leslie and Cristina. As usual, the three girls laugh when they see me. They always laugh when they see me. I should have a complex, but I don't.

"Hey!" Taryn yells to me. "Way to ditch me this morning!"

I almost blurt, "Hey, loser, I did not ditch you!" Instead I shove my hands into my pockets. "Let's just get out of here," I say. "Sixth grade. Day one is over and out. Just like me."

I'm glad I didn't start a fight. After that, Taryn giggles and waves good-bye to her friends. Then we leave Leslie and Cristina standing there and walk down to the lobby of the new building. There are two buses back to our neighborhood each day. I want to be on the first one.

"Sorry about this morning," I mumble as we walk along. I feel extra bad when I see that the skid mark is still visible on her pink shirt.

"Thanks," Taryn mumbles back. "How was your first day at Westcott?"

"Wack," I say. "What about you?"

She grins. "Excellent," she says proudly.

Taryn starts to tell me all about her day. I expect to hear some outrageous story. She's good at making up stories. But her day doesn't sound that much different than mine. Same forms, same grind.

As we're walking along, I spy a huge poster on the wall.

"Look at that!" I cry, stopping in my tracks.

The poster has a list of sports team tryouts. There's the word SOCCER in bright blue letters at the very top of the list. I pump my fist in the air and let out a loud hoot.

"Wow," Taryn says. "Jeff, you will *so* make the team. I know it."

I pull out my notebook and pencil and jot down the soccer team tryout times I need to know.

"Maybe I should play soccer this year, too," Taryn says.

I chuckle. "You're kidding, right?"

When I say that, Taryn pokes me in the arm — hard. Then she keeps right on poking and talking, giving me a dozen reasons why she can too play soccer, and how I'm some kind of super-ogre to say that she can't.

Of course I didn't mean that at all. I was just kidding around.

Sometimes that girl can talk and talk and talk

and rather than try to keep up, it's so much better to just keep my mouth shut.

Kids rush past us on all sides, racing to their buses or to cars idling in the parking lot. Another bell rings as we push through the main doors into the real world. What do all these bells mean, anyway? It's like some kind of foreign language. I hope I learn it fast. A few yards away, over at our bus stop, I see Peter and Anthony. We race over, and the four of us (including Taryn) decide to sit at the back of the bus on the way home, just like we did that morning.

I make sure Taryn is sitting before the bus moves so she doesn't fall again.

The bus lurches toward home and I peer out the window. Rows of green trees flash by. There's a lot of traffic this afternoon. A warm breeze blows in. It smells like a combination of mowed grass and car exhaust.

All around me, everyone's talking at the same time, buzzing about the first day of school. I really want to join in the conversation, but my brain stalls. All I can think about is the soccer tryouts. If I get on the soccer team, everything about sixth grade will just fall into place.

At least I hope it will.

Fingers crossed.

Chapter 5

❀ ❀ ❀ TARYN ❀ ❀ ❀

Love Note

I dig my purple-painted toes into my plush, swirly bedroom carpet and just streeeeeetch.

Good morning, sunshine.

I'm so ready for day two of sixth grade. I'm even looking forward to getting some real homework. Jeff would laugh if he heard me say that one. He complained nonstop yesterday about those diagnostic tests we all have to take this week. Ever since we were teeny he's hated tests.

The only bad part about today happens after four o'clock. That's when Mom drives me over to Dr. Wexler's office, where he'll torture me and make me read E's, R's, and Z's from some chart. Today's YIGG-Day, as in "Yikes! I'm Getting Glasses!" Day.

It's the day Dr. Wexler confirms my worst suspicions about my bad eyes and tells me what kind of glasses I need. My brother Tim says I'll have to get thick ones that look like the bottom of a soda bottle. Of course, Tim's just trying to scare me. I think.

Mew, mew, meeeeew.

My cat, Zsa-Zsa, purrs and presses her back against my legs. She does figure eights, and her tail flashes in and out between the crooks of my knees. Of course it's nearly impossible to pull on a skirt when she's doing this, but I try anyway. I'm always up for a challenge. Besides, I selected the best possible day-two outfit, and I'm dying to try it on right now.

L and C helped me choose outfit number two. Last night after school ended and we all took our different buses home, the three of us talked on the phone with three-way calling.

Cristina told me today that she wants to be my fashion advisor. She didn't witness my fall on the bus, but she did see me in school wearing a shirt with this HUGE black mark on it, and she said it was a *faux pas*. That's French for "embarrassing mess," I think. Truthfully, I didn't look like I fell on a bus. I looked like I was *run over* by a bus. Jeff even told me how awful I looked. He and his friends laughed for hours. Well, for a few minutes, anyway.

Apparently, Cristina says I need an outfit that will make everyone forget yesterday's skid mark. So I decided on something girly for today: my peasant skirt, teal tee, and these brown sandals with the little gold buckles that I got at an end-of-summer sale. Plus, I'm wearing a new ponytail holder, too, with the ribbons that flow down the back. Cristina begged me to wear my hair down, but I just cringed. I am happy to change my skirt. I am happy to change my top. But when it comes to my hair, there are some things that will never, ever change.

I break my own record getting ready for school. I'm dressed, combed, and cherry-vanilla lip-glossed in only fifteen minutes. Dad is there, sitting in the kitchen reading his morning paper. I kiss him, Mom, and Zsa-Zsa good-bye. Then it's off to Jeff's house so we can hightail it to the bus stop. We alternate pickup days. Yesterday he came here; today, I'm going there.

When I knock on the Rasmussens' door, I hear Toots bark. Then the lock clicks open.

"Hello!" Jeff's mother greets me warmly.

I grin. "Hey," I say. "Can you tell Jeff I'm here?"

Mrs. Rasmussen puts a finger up to her chin, like she's thinking extra-hard.

"Oh," she says. "Jeff isn't here, Taryn. Didn't he tell you?"

Inside my new sandals, I feel my toes curl.

Tell me what? That he's an undercover agent on special assignment and he's been transferred to Siberia? That he's decided to drop out of sixth grade after only one day? What?

"Jeff got a ride with his stepfather this morning," Mrs. Rasmussen said. "Mr. Rasmussen brought him over to school early so Jeff could meet the soccer coach. You know Jeff — eager beaver!"

"Oh, yeah," I say, backing away from the door just a little bit. "He said something. . . ." But I just trail off.

Just then, Toots crosses the threshold, tail wagging like a windshield wiper, back and forth, forth and back. He recognizes me and sniffs my ankles.

"Thanks, anyway," I say, bending down to pet Toots. I back down the front porch steps and head for the bus stop — alone.

For some reason, the bus stop is way less crowded today than it was yesterday. Then I realize why: I'm ten minutes early. Everything about today started off in order but now I'm getting nervous. Something is off. I glance down at my shirt and sandals to make sure that at least my outfit is still in good shape. I need to count on that.

Before long, the usual suspects show up, one-by-one. Then the bus rolls up.

Peter and Anthony wave to me from the back of the bus like yesterday, but I don't want to sit there without Jeff. Emma says hello, too, but I just force a smile and keep walking. I spot an empty row in the middle of the bus and park my peasant skirt there. No one sits next to me, but I'm right behind the eighth-grade twins. They're laughing during the whole ride and I can't help wondering if they're laughing at me — or my skirt — or my sandals — or *worse*?

When I stare out the bus window, everything looks fuzzy, which reminds me of my eye doctor appointment. My stomach churns at the thought of Dr. Wexler's icy fingertips as he clicks the levers on the testing equipment.

Lucky for me, I forget about all that the moment the bus pulls into the cul-de-sac at school. L and C are standing right there, waiting for me.

I love my best friends.

"Taryn!" Leslie yells. Her yellow-blond hair is pulled up on top of her head and she's wearing this off-white, striped sundress that accentuates her tan. I guess she really meant it when she said she wanted to get a boyfriend this year. As I race over toward her, I notice a group of seventh grade boys staring her way.

"That outfit looks A-plus, awesome," Cristina says, as if she had not only counseled me on what to wear, but had actually come into my closet and dressed me that morning.

I beam proudly. "Thanks for your help," I say. I'm so grateful not to have a skid mark anywhere on my clothes today.

Cristina throws her arm around my shoulder and the row of bangles on her arm makes a clanking noise. She's wearing a pale green, long-sleeved T-shirt and flared jeans (black, of course) with zigzag stitching on the leg. We all have such different styles, but we look good walking along together as a threesome.

"So where's Jeff?" Leslie asks, looking around.

"He's already here, somewhere in the gym, I think," I answer. "Something about soccer. He got a ride to school early."

"If Jeff makes the middle-school team," Cristina says, "he'll be a part of the popular pack with all the older kids."

"Oh, get real!" I say. It's hard to imagine Jeff being in any kind of pack, let alone the *popular* kind.

"Knowing Jeff, that'll give him a really big head," Leslie adds.

"Speaking of which . . ." Cristina lowers her voice to a whisper. "Did you see Emma Wallace yesterday? She has a *huge* head, doesn't she?"

"It's just a different hairstyle," I say. "She's wearing barrettes, so you can see more of her face."

I don't mean to defend Emma, but that's the way it comes out.

"Yeah, well, I think she looks like one of those bobblehead dolls," Leslie says.

We all crack up at the word *bobblehead*.

"She takes my bus, you know," I add.

"I forgot," Leslie says. "She lives near you. That's such a drag."

It's really not a big deal, but I play along. "Yeah," I say. "It's hard living near Little Miss Perfect."

I can't really remember when the three of us decided to hate Emma Wallace, but we definitely made a calculated decision to do it. It would be easy to explain — and understand — if Emma were some kind of super-witch with flaming tornado hair and a flying broomstick. But she doesn't *have* any of those things.

Nope, Emma never has messy hair. Her perfectly placed, silver flower hair clips never change position, as opposed to my clips, which move around and get tangled in every possible strand of hair. She also has perfect nails, painted a different shade of pink each week, usually to match her socks. In addition to the perfect hair, nails, and clothes, Emma walks like she's on some kind of runway. It's more of a strut, really. I think she looks like a model when she does that, but Leslie always compares Emma to a rooster or some other kind of farm bird.

I know the bird comparison is unfair. And it's not like we *want* to be mean or nasty about Emma. We know she's one of the sweetest kids in our class, not to mention the smartest. She's always the teacher's first pick. She's always the one getting straight A's, even in gym class. And she pretends like work doesn't matter, but then she always asks for extra credit. No one person should be so pretty and so *perfect*. TLC vs. Emma is just the way it's always been; I guess it's the way it will always be.

Since Leslie, Cristina, and I are all in the same homeroom, we were assigned lockers near each other. As we enter school, the three of us shuffle through the crowd of kids toward our yellow locker bank.

"Hey, Taryn," Leslie says, squeezing my arm. "What's *that*?"

I spot a piece of paper poking out from the slat in my locker.

Cristina plucks it out before I can. She starts to unfold it.

"Ooooh!" Cristina coos. "Is it a love note?"

I roll my eyes. "It is not," I say, snatching the note from her fingers. Without even looking at it, I shove it into my bag.

"You're not going to open it?" Leslie asks. "Who is it from?"

I shake my head. "How should I know?" I reply.

"You have to open it!" Cristina says, reaching for my bag. She tugs and I tug back. My bag swings into a group of kids walking by.

"Watch it!" a tall boy growls. He says something else but I can't hear what it is.

"Moron," Leslie says, but he's already out of earshot when she says it.

A bell rings and we all flash one another a look. L and C open their own lockers fast. None of us have much in our lockers yet, since it's only the second day of school, but we each go through the motions: turning the dials, pretending to forget our combinations, doing it all over again, and then clicking the metal doors shut. In my bag, I have a dozen photos, postcards, and other stuff to decorate the inside of my locker. I know what I'm going to hang front and center: a photo strip of TLC from the beach this summer. We're all wearing movie-star sunglasses and posing with kissy-faces, like something from some magazine.

Before heading into homeroom, I get permission to go to the girls' bathroom. I head into one of the stalls with my bag. That's when I pull out the mystery note.

I'm surprised to see that it's Jeff's scrawl inside. I told Jeff my locker number yesterday, but I'm amazed he remembered it. He probably can't even remember his *own* locker number.

Hey T,

Sorry I forgot to tell u about soccer. See u in class or meet me after school for the tryouts!!! It's on Field B. Bring L & C if you want. LOL.

Bye, Jeff

A grin spreads across my face. I knew Jeff hadn't blown me off. Good friends never, ever, *ever* do that.

Quickly, I stuff the note back into the pocket of my bag, zip it, and duck out of the stall. Homeroom is starting and I don't want to be late.

As I head into the now-empty middle school hallway, I breathe a sigh of relief.

Somehow, I'll figure out how to finish up the school day, get to Jeff's soccer tryout, *and* still make it to Dr. Wexler's.

And somehow day two of sixth grade won't be so bad after all.

Chapter 6

• • • Jeff • • •

Beyond a Reasonable Doubt

I feel like someone just handed me a bazillion bucks. I'm standing in the middle of the field, cleats on, with the rest of the soccer team wannabes. Westcott takes soccer very seriously. This district has produced more champions than any other school district. And I could be a part of all that.

If that isn't the biggest *whoa* of all time, then what is?

I wish the air wasn't so sticky right now. Summer is supposed to be over, but today is another scorcher. Of course, Coach Byrnes also made us do ten laps before tryouts, so that could explain some of the heat.

Coach has assembled us on the field, awaiting further instructions. That sounds like secret agent talk to me. I know it isn't, but my imagination is going crazy.

At least waiting gives me a solid minute to catch my breath.

My pulse thumps.

While we're waiting, I scan the bleacher seats for a familiar face. I see lots of kids, but only a few from my new class. Peter decided not to try out for the team this year, but he still came to root for me. And Anthony doesn't even like soccer, but he also came. I see some girls I know, too, like Emma Wallace and Leslie Smart and this other girl with red hair who I met in homeroom this morning.

The one person I don't see is Taryn. She'd better get here soon to cheer me on. I left a note in her locker. What's her problem?

Coach Byrnes toots his whistle and lines us up in front of this orange-cone obstacle course. I can ace this drill. I know it.

The whistle blows and we're off, passing and receiving. I trap the ball perfectly and set up for a return pass.

"Fine job!" Coach Byrnes says with a smile as I trot around him and back to the line. I clap my hands together and glance back out at the bleachers.

Peter and Anthony spot my look.

"Go, man, go!" they clap. I throw my arm into the air, wishing they could be out here with me. Right now, no one else on the field wants to talk to me. It's a weird feeling.

Why can't I see Taryn? Is she sitting down somewhere, out of sight?

"Rasmussen!"

I hear my last name and dart over toward Coach Byrnes and his assistant. For my next test, they're setting me up for a one-on-one with this huge eighth grader named Walt. I'll play offense. Walt is defense.

I catch my breath again. This is my big chance to make a goal and prove myself.

With one swift move, I take possession of the soccer ball, dribble it to the side, and step into a wide kick. There's a loud *plock* as the ball explodes right off the side of my foot and fires directly into the goal.

Walt stands there, stunned. No one can believe I made such an easy goal, least of all me. Coach Byrnes asks me to "hang back" while he chats with Walt. Then the coach has me line up again. I can't believe it. Now he wants to match me up with this other older kid named Will. Since I'm just a lowly sixth grader, I have to prove myself and my soccer abilities beyond a reasonable doubt.

So I line up, take more deep breaths, and prepare for another goal. That's when Coach Byrnes pulls a bait and switch. He makes me play defense instead.

I race over in front of the net, bouncing on my toes. I'm expecting a shot to the right or left or way over my head. Will looks like one of those cartoon bulls, digging one foot into the ground, head down, eyes glued on me. I half expect him to start snorting.

Coach Byrnes blows the whistle, and Will charges.

I take a hop to the left. Of course, Will kicks to the right.

Swoosh.

I can practically feel the air as the ball flies past my head, right into the goal.

The bleachers erupt in applause. I hang my head down, figuring that I blew my chance. But I'm wrong. Coach Byrnes comes up to me and slaps me on the back.

"You've got a lot of potential," he says.

I'm waiting for the bad news, but it doesn't come.

"I think you'd make a great addition to the team."

Did I hear him correctly? Did he just say what I think he said?

"Of course," Coach continued, "I need to mull things over. I'll be posting the team list later this week, but I'm very glad you came to tryouts, Jeff. You know, we don't usually take sixth graders on this team. That's what the sixth-grade team was formed for, but I think you may be one of the exceptions. . . ."

Coach Byrnes wags his finger at me and walks away. With all the attention, I feel like I'm on some kind of imaginary trampoline, totally airborne. My head swings around toward the bleachers again, searching for Taryn. I don't know why it matters so much to me to know she's out there. But it does.

Finally, I spot her. She waves to me from the end of a row where she's standing with Leslie and Cristina. I wave back.

After we finish a few additional drills for Coach Byrnes and company, we're dismissed. I jog off the field.

"Way to go!" Taryn cheers from the sidelines. "I'm so sorry I was late, but I was finishing something after class and then I had to call my mom and —"

"It's okay," I say, interrupting her.

"Did you make the team?" Cristina asks, flipping her dark hair. I don't know why that girl always dresses so weird. Who wears black all the time?

Peter and Anthony have come over by now, too. Anthony puts me in a choke hold and plants a noogie on my head. It's just something we do.

The girls back off a little, but then I spot Peter staring at Leslie. I know he thinks she's cute, but he's way too shy to admit it. He said once this summer that he likes her blond hair. We made fun of him, so he hasn't mentioned it since.

"So what are you guys doing now?" Leslie asks.

"Celebrating," I say, giving each of the guys a double high five.

"My mom isn't picking me up for a half hour," Cristina says.

"Mine, neither. Let's go down to the park for a while," Anthony suggests.

In fifth grade, we always hung out together. Now that we're in a different school, there are more places to hang. Just down the street is a town park with old trees, built-in chessboards, and swings.

"I don't know," I mutter. "I'm feeling kind of tired. I got up at five this morning. But I can take the late bus, I guess."

"Forget the bus, Jeff. My mom will give you a ride. Let's all go," Peter says.

61

"Um . . ." Cristina crosses her arms. "I don't exactly feel like going to the *playground*," she says sarcastically.

Anthony rolls his eyes. "Then don't."

"I wish I could go," Taryn says. "But I have an appointment this afternoon at four."

Taryn's been talking about this big appointment for weeks. She has to go to the eye doctor. Last year she started getting these eye aches. Sometimes she can't even see the TV.

As we're standing there, Taryn pulls out her turquoise cell phone case and dials her mother's number to make sure she's on the way.

While Taryn's talking to her mom, no one says much, and no one moves. An eternity passes before we make any move toward the parking lot — or the park. As we're standing there, I'm starting to suspect that maybe Leslie thinks Peter is cute in the same way he thinks she's cute. She keeps staring at him. Peter is acting even goofier than usual.

"What are we doing here?" Anthony finally blurts.

"Yeah, let's motor," I say to everyone. "Let me just get my bag and change."

I head into the locker room to switch into a non-sweaty shirt and take off my soccer cleats. By the time I come out, Taryn's mother has pulled up in her SUV.

"Yo, guys," I call out, making a snap decision when I see the free ride. "I think I'm just going to hitch with Taryn."

"Hitch?" Anthony says. "I thought you said you wanted to hang."

"Naw, I'm too beat," I say.

"Okay," Peter says, "I guess it's just the four of us, then."

"Whatever," I nod. "Call me later, gators."

The girls say their good-byes and I bid my buddies so long, too. Then I follow Taryn over to her mother's car and take a seat in the back.

The floor is covered with crunched-up paper cups, crumpled notepaper, Kleenex, and other junk. If there's one absolute in the universe, it's this: The Taylor car is always a mess. Taryn's mother usually blames Tim, Tom, or Todd. I think there's still dirt on the floor from five years ago.

"Buckle up, kids," Mrs. Taylor announces after saying hello. She's such a stickler for rules.

"Mom, did you know that Jeff probably just made the soccer team and it is SUCH a big deal? Sixth graders never make it," Taryn says.

"Well, congratulations, Jeff," Mrs. Taylor says to me.

I happily accept the compliment — and I know she means it, too. Taryn's mom has watched me play soccer in our backyards since I could walk.

"I'll drive you home before I take Taryn to the doctor, Jeff," Mrs. Taylor says.

"Thanks," I say.

The SUV tires squeal as we pull out of the parking area.

"I just knew you'd make the team," Taryn says to me. She pokes me in the arm, but this time it's friendlier than usual. For once, she's not trying to inflict a bruise.

"Anything good happen at school today?" I ask her, trying to make polite conversation. After all, we are in the car with her mom.

"Nothing major," Taryn says. "Took that reading test, put some pictures up in my locker . . ."

"Whoop-dee-doo."

"What's wrong with a little interior decorating?" Taryn asks.

"I tried out for soccer. What did you try out for?" I ask.

Taryn makes a face. "Nothing. Yet."

"You said you would. What about photography club, or maybe the newspaper? Did you see the school carnival sign-up sheet?" I ask. "It was posted outside every classroom."

"Yes, I saw it," Taryn says. "But . . ."

Her voice trails off.

"But *what*?" I say.

"But . . . I don't know . . . I just didn't sign up. End of story."

"You would make the best carnival leader, T. And they need some people from every grade," I say. "Maybe *I'll* sign you up."

She thinks I'm serious and overreacts. It's such a Taryn thing to do.

"Don't you dare sign me up, Jeff!" she wails.

"Why not?" I say, still teasing her a little. "If I do soccer and you do the carnival, then we'd both be a part of something."

"Just not the same thing," Taryn says.

We're quiet for a minute, and I can see Taryn's face gets pale. She goes from jabbering to nothing in ten seconds. She's definitely thinking about the eye doctor now.

"Taryn," I say. "Don't freak. It's just the eye guy. How bad can it be?"

"Jeff, you have no idea. Dr. Wexler's breath reeks. I'll bet he's going to make me blink a hundred times or dislodge my eyeball or pluck out my eyelashes or make me read something that is just too far away and then he's going to tell me that I need to wear awful, ugly glasses for the rest of my life!"

Taryn's mom glances at us in the rearview mirror.

"Taryn?" she says. "We're not even there yet. Could you please cut the dramatics?"

It's hard not to chuckle at that, especially when Taryn is acting like a true drama queen.

Taryn doesn't say anything else. She just glares.

All I can think about now is what Taryn said. I visualize Dr. Wexler plucking eyelashes or ripping out eyeballs like in some kind of bad horror movie. I can't help but laugh out loud. Lucky for me, Mrs. Taylor doesn't hear. And Taryn is too worried to pay attention to me now. Within a few minutes, we've pulled into my driveway.

Unlucky for me, my half sister, Blair, is on our porch with Toots — and she's got the sparkly barrettes on his ears again. "Good luck," I say to Taryn, climbing out of the car.

"Good-*bye*," Taryn replies, sticking out her tongue.

Chapter 7

❀ ❀ ❀ TARYN ❀ ❀ ❀

Bizarre

I can't believe it.

Yesterday confirmed a sad fact: I really do need glasses! When I could barely identify the enormous, fuzzy E at the top of the eye chart, Dr. Wexler wrote me a prescription right there on the spot. He claims I have something called astigmatism. It sounds painful, but it isn't. At least not yet.

But I can't think about that right now. It's time for my first school carnival meeting. The sky-blue sheet of paper taped to the door of room 12C reads SCHOOL CARNIVAL MEETING, HERE, 2:45 P.M., so I know I'm in the right place.

Of course I have to stand on my tiptoes to read it.

It's already 2:35 and there's a line up and down the hallway, but the teacher hasn't even unlocked the door yet. I recognize a few other kids from my English and social studies classes, but none of my good friends are here. Leslie is more into drama club, and today is Cristina's first day of tennis. There are some older kids from my neighborhood here, but I don't recognize anyone else. I notice this one girl, leaning up against the wall. She has long brown hair like me, but it's down, flowing around her shoulders. She's reading a book. Then she looks up and sees me.

"Hey, are you here for the carnival sign-up?" she asks me.

I nod and smile, not knowing what to say. My brother Todd always says, "When in doubt, smile." Todd's a huge dork, but he's really smart about some things.

"This is my third year doing this," the girl says.

"Wow," I reply. I could have come up with something better than that, couldn't I?

"I'm Valerie, but you can call me Val. Who are you?"

"Taryn," I manage to say.

"Cool name," Val says. "So, what — are you a sixer?"

I assume she means sixth grader. I just nod

again. And smile. My cheeks ache from smiling so much these first three days of school.

Everything about Val screams "cool" without trying too hard, and about six different people say hello and wave to her. When Val looks at me, I notice how her eyes are this crystal green color, a lot like my cat Zsa-Zsa's eyes. Val's one-hundred-percent color-coordinated, too. She's even carrying a notebook marked "Carnival" that matches the trim on her T-shirt.

As we're standing there, a teacher shows up, waddling to the door. The way he has his sleeves rolled up makes his arms look like little, hairy sausages. Beads of sweat drip from his forehead. He opens the lock with a grimace and a groan, like he's lifting something heavy.

"I'm so sorry to be late, kids. Please file in and take a seat," he says, mopping his brow with a handkerchief. "I'm Mr. Wood."

Something about the harried expression on Mr. Wood's face says to me, "Do NOT mess around, or you'll be sorry." I shuffle my sandals inside and smile (of course), even though, at the same time, I'm desperately trying *not* to make eye contact. Not that it would matter with my lousy eyes.

"Don't get freaked out by Mr. Wood," Val whispers to me. "He's a total sweetie."

Although I have a hard time believing that any teacher can be classified as "sweetie," I believe Val. She seems to know everyone — and everything — at Westcott. I can tell. Although I'd like more than anything to sit with her, Val disappears off to one side. I head for the back of the room.

It's lonely in the back by the radiator, all by myself.

What am I doing here? Have I made a terrible mistake? I'm just about to get up and slip right back out into the hall when I see Val. She gives me this smile and for some reason, it keeps me glued to my seat.

I have to give this whole carnival thing a chance. After all, I promised myself I would. I promised Jeff, too.

I am happy to see that as soon as Mr. Wood drops his large canvas bag onto the teacher's desk his frown melts and he actually cracks a few jokes. Then he's writing something up on the board.

I squint to read the bold purple letters: BEACH PARTY.

"What can I say? I am very, very, VERY excited about this year's carnival," Mr. Wood announces. He's not so out of breath anymore; clapping his hands together like a little kid. I glance around

70

the room and realize that everyone else seems genuinely excited, just like Mr. Wood. Even Val is clapping her hands together.

Maybe this *will* be fun?

Fun. Fun. Fun. I repeat the word, as if saying something a hundred times can make it true.

"Parents, teachers, and our entire community have gotten behind this carnival," Mr. Wood explains. He goes on to tell us that any money earned during the carnival will be used to purchase special things for Westcott *and* for a local organization that helps orphans.

I had no idea that this was all for such a good — no, *great* — cause.

Mr. Wood tells us how we'll be renting a dunk tank for the carnival (to dunk the teachers, we all hope!), and that the local newspaper will be covering the event. Everyone who participates will get their name mentioned in the Lifestyle section.

Okay. That settles it.

Now I'm totally in.

Even though most of the planning for the carnival has already taken place, including equipment rental, food purchasing, ticket mailings, and more, they still need students to volunteer their time. The school needs as many kids as possible to help out once the carnival begins. And Mr. Wood wants to find a few good carnival leaders, too. That's where we come in.

When he asks for leader wannabes, my hand shoots right up like a rocket. Jeff would probably say that's because I like to be in charge. He's always telling me that I'm too bossy. He's wrong. Across the room, I see Val's got her hand high in the air, too.

"Goodness!" Mr. Wood cries as he looks out at the roomful of volunteers. Then he asks us each to jot down our names and a few sentences about why we'd like to be a leader. I wish I had more time, but I scribble the first things that come to mind — that I'm organized, responsible, full of energy, and really want to be involved in a good cause. By the time Mr. Wood collects our pages and reads them over, I realize that I've been holding my breath.

Breathe, Taryn, breathe.

I hope I don't pass out.

Finally, Mr. Wood starts calling out names. He picks Valerie — of course. Then he says the two words I am dying to hear most: Taryn Taylor. He's called on *me* to be a carnival team leader. I get to oversee the "activity zone," an area of the carnival devoted to games like ring toss and the fake fishing pond. I'm in charge of the whole cluster of sixth-grade volunteers chosen to run those games.

That can't be too hard, can it?

Taryn Taylor, Team Leader.

I love the sound of that.

Mr. Wood starts talking about the different activities that are planned, and we all throw out ideas to make them even better. There are going to be balloons made in the shape of ocean animals, and a sand-covered obstacle course. Val suggests a spinning Wheel of Fortune with beachy prizes, like sunglasses and Frisbees. Wow. She has some great ideas. I'm impressed. Then I see Val has her notebook open; she's writing down all these notes.

Following Val's lead, I pull out a piece of yellow-lined paper from my backpack and scribble a long to-do list. I've barely begun, but I'm already behind.

1. Balloon animals? Who can make them?
2. Bean bag throw (waves) — how many bags?
3. Obstacle course — do we need extra sand?
4. Soda bottle toss — get 20 rings from . . . someone?
5. Make a bizarre to sell arts & crafts for extra $$$

At some point, I glance up at the clock on the wall and realize that while we've been talking and brainstorming an hour has gone by.

It is now 4:06.

Just then, Mr. Wood realizes the time, too.

"Oh, dear!" he cries. "How did it get so late?"

"Don't worry, Mr. Wood," Val calls out. "We're cool."

"Thanks, Valerie. It just goes to show you . . . what a great big undertaking this all is . . . and how enthusiastic we all are and . . ."

By now, everyone is hauling their backpacks onto shoulders and making a beeline for the door. That's when Mr. Wood hollers, "HOLD ON RIGHT THERE, KIDS!"

Val, me, and the others kids stop dead in our tracks. Flailing his arms, Mr. Wood jumps in front of the door before anyone can leave.

"Just one more thing before you go, volunteers," he shouts. "Our next meeting will take place here in room twelve C on Monday after school, so bring all of your best beach party ideas with you then. Have a nice weekend!"

Finally, he releases the door latch. We're free.

Despite the weirdness of Mr. Wood's acrobatic act, I feel this jolt of positive energy about the whole carnival experience. Jeff was right. Being a carnival team leader is good for me. I can't wait to tell — and thank — him.

On the way out, Val bumps into me. "See you Monday," she blurts as she rushes past. I see her link arms with another friend a few feet away and then she's gone.

I head to my locker to grab my stuff and wait for Cristina. Her dad is giving us a ride home since she had to stay late for tennis practice.

When Cristina doesn't show up right away, I head for the basement gym area, but she's not there, either. Although I'm getting used to Westcott, I still feel a little bit lost. Where *is* everyone? It doesn't help matters that everything I see is a blur, so as I'm walking around panic sets in and I feel increasingly, totally *alone.* Maybe I should call Tim or Tom to pick me up. They're annoying, but at least they're reliably annoying. If they weren't, Mom would yell at them.

I take a seat on one of the locker room benches and then, magically, Cristina appears from behind a bank of red lockers.

"I've been searching for you everywhere, T!" C cries as soon as she spots me. "I've been all over the building, which is pretty tough because I don't know where anything is and tennis got out a half hour ago —"

"Wait! I was looking for you, too," I say, interrupting. "The carnival meeting ran a little long and I couldn't find you, but I —"

"Hold up, hold up," Cristina says, poking her arms into the air with a *clinkety-clank*.

I notice she's wearing white shorts and a T-shirt that says WESTCOTT TENNIS on this tiny pocket, but she still wears her favorite (and noisy) bangles and dangly earrings. Cristina always says that the clothes are the worst part of playing tennis. She'd prefer cool, black Nike outfits like Serena Williams, rather than the boring tennis whites everyone expects. Leslie and I figure that Cristina will end up being some edgy fashion designer one day.

I secretly hope that wish comes true. Then I could get free, cool clothes for life.

"I'm sorry, Cris," I say at least ten times in a row without taking a breath.

"Okay, okay, I forgive you," Cristina says, grabbing me in a bear hug. "I literally just called Dad, and he's on his way over now, so it's cool, *plus* it's Friday. . . ."

We grab our bags and head for the front doors. There's a pickup and drop-off area at the edge of the parking lot. Outside, it isn't chilly at all. I stuff my jacket into my bag.

When Cristina's dad finally arrives, my stomach is rumbling like a volcano. I should have eaten more at lunch.

I wonder what culinary surprise Mom will have waiting when I get home. Cristina knows all about Mom's kitchen experiments. One time when she visited this summer, Mom made shrimp toast. At least that was what Mom called it. It tasted more like fish cardboard. Gross. We each had to drink at least twelve glasses of lemonade to get that taste out of our mouths.

"So, was tennis fun?" I ask Cristina as we both climb into the back seat.

She grins at me so widely that I can see the edges of her retainer.

"I think I might even get a top spot on the team," Cristina says, nodding. "A couple of the older kids are good, but I'm just as good. I'm psyched."

"Wow," I mumble, impressed.

"What about you? Does the school carnival sound good?" Cristina asks.

"Really good," I say with a nod. "I'm sooooo glad I signed up. The theme is Beach Party."

"Too hot!" Cristina says. "You should have a tanning booth."

"You wish," I reply. "My brother would love that, too."

"I can't believe that the first week of sixth grade is over already," Cristina says.

"Yeah." I sigh. "What do you think is the most different thing about this year so far?"

Cristina laughs and covers her mouth. "Cute boys," she whispers.

Now I know she's officially boy-crazy.

When her dad drops me off in front of our house, Cristina yells, "Shotgun!" and hops into the front seat of his car. "Call me later!" she yells through the window.

Her dad honks and she waves as they drive off.

I walk up to my front door.

"I didn't think you'd ever get home," a voice calls out from behind our bushes. Then a familiar head pops up. It's Jeff. "I've been on my porch forever, T. So what's up?"

He stands there with his baseball glove on one hand, and a baseball in the other.

"What's up with you?" I ask.

"You know what I mean. How was the carnival meeting?" Jeff asks, stepping closer to me. "Was I right or was I right? Cool after-school thing for you, right?"

I give him a familiar grin. "Cool — as ice," I say. "You were right."

"Of course, I'm always right!" Jeff shouts. He

bursts into some kind of maniacal laughter that projects him across the lawn and back onto the sidewalk. I look up the street to make sure no one is watching.

"Shhhh," I say. "You're embarrassing yourself."

"Nah, I'm embarrassing *you*," Jeff says, laughing even louder.

I chase after him. We end up at my front steps again and plop down, still laughing.

"So what happened in your classes today?" I ask.

"You saw me like ten times in the hall at school," Jeff says.

"I know, but that was this morning."

"Classes were fine. Whatever. Math is going to be tough. You saw the list, right?"

"What list?"

"It's official. I made the soccer team. Coach Byrnes posted it at lunchtime."

I feel like lunging at Jeff to give him a great big bear hug. But of course I don't. He'd freak.

"Congratulations!" I cry. "You deserve it, Jeff."

"I know," Jeff says, slapping his knees. "I rock!"

Of course I'm proud of him, even though he's acting a little braggy. But I guess I would be braggy, too. Making the team in sixth grade is a very big deal, after all.

"Hey, what's that?" Jeff asks me out of the blue. He points to my chin. "Eww. Disgust-o!"

"What?" I ask nervously, reaching up to wipe my face. But there's nothing there.

"Gotcha!" Jeff says with one of his satisfied smirks.

"Very funny," I grumble.

"I know!" Jeff exclaims. Then he moves to get up and head back to his house.

"Wait!" I cry. "I almost forgot to tell you about something I saw in the newspaper this morning. Something huge."

"Since when do you read the newspaper?" Jeff says.

"Since forever," I reply, not mentioning that I usually just read the entertainment section. "Don't you want to hear what it was?"

"Okay. What?"

I make a loud drumroll sound, getting down on my knee for dramatic effect.

"Next week, Floyd Flannigan is coming to the bookstore downtown," I say.

Jeff's jaw nearly hits the steps.

"No way!" he exclaims. But I see anticipation bubble up inside of him like soda fizz. He stands up. "I don't believe it!"

"Believe it," I say. "He'll be there next Wednesday."

Ever since we could read, Jeff and I declared ourselves mega-fans of a fantasy writer named Floyd Flannigan. He's a hundred-year-old Irish guy who writes these incredible, amazing, fantastical books called the Outer Space Chronicles. Jeff and I have each read the entire collection of his books at least three times. On his Web site, fans of his books are called Floyd Fanatics.

That's me and Jeff all the way.

"He's coming HERE?!" Jeff screams. "That's INCREDIBLE!"

It's quiet outside, so everything we say echoes up and down the street. My brother Todd steps out onto our porch to check out the racket.

"Yo, Taryn, Jeff," Todd says in his I'm-the-older-brother-and-I-know-so-much-better-than-you-do voice. "Someone's gonna call the police if you guys don't quiet down."

"No one's going to call the police," I bark back. "Give me a break."

"Mom's the one who sent me out here," Todd says. "So why don't you just keep it down?"

"Fine," I snap.

"Uh . . . sorry, Todd," Jeff gulps, throwing his

hands into the air in surrender. As soon as Todd goes back inside, Jeff turns to me and whispers, "Floyd Fanatics unite! We totally have to go."

"Totally," I agree. "Let's make a plan. I can get one of my *other* brothers to take us."

Jeff nods. Then he ducks back toward his house. I know the Todd incident scared him off. For whatever reason, Jeff always gets intimidated by my older brothers.

As soon as I step inside my house, Todd walks by and makes this crinkly face.

"That kid is a bozo," he says.

"He's my friend," I say.

"Yeah, well you're a bozo, too."

"Moooooom!" I call.

"What is it now?" Mom asks, appearing from around the corner. "I heard you and Jeff outside. How was day three? Tell me everything. Everything!"

I expect her to yank me all the way into the kitchen for further interrogation and maybe some late afternoon food experimentation, too, but no, she just wants to relax. We collapse together onto the sofa in our living room.

By now I've forgotten all about tattling on Todd. Instead, I tell Mom about the new teachers I met today, the book report I have to do for English class, and then I talk about volunteering for the school carnival. She looks excited about all of my news. I even show her my to-do list from the meeting.

"What a big job! This all looks very cool," Mom says as she reads the list. "Wait. What's that?" She points to the last item. "Bizarre? Like . . . *strange*?"

"No, no," I insist. "It's bizarre like a flea market. You know. *Bizarre*."

"Oh, Taryn!" Mom's eyes glisten and she smiles. "You mean the word 'bazaar,' don't you? With three A's."

"Oh, yeah. Whoops."

I quickly scratch off the misspelled word and rewrite it the way Mom says to.

As I do, Mom laughs and tousles my hair. Sometimes when she does that I feel like a baby all over again. And right now, for some reason, I don't mind so much. I inhale a whiff of her perfume, and everything seems just right in the world.

"Bazaar," I say the word slowly, a little embarrassed, trying to emphasize the A's so I don't get it wrong ever again.

I may be starting off sixth grade with a bang, but my spelling still needs some serious help.

Maybe I should spend the weekend locked in my bedroom with a dictionary?

Like *that's* ever going to happen.

Chapter 8

• • • Jeff • • •

The Soccer Table

"How was your weekend?" Anthony asks as we stroll into the cafeteria with Peter.

"Boring," I groan. "But J.D. got me a new portable goal for soccer. We set it up in the backyard."

"Nice!" Peter says. "Your old net had all those holes."

We stop at the lunchroom bulletin board and check out the specials for the day.

"What do you think they really put in Browned Meat Loaf Surprise?" I wonder out loud.

"Meat," Anthony says.

"And loaf," Peter adds.

I grab my stomach and pretend to laugh at their

dumb joke. Then I motor inside the lunchroom and grab a bright blue, jet-washed tray.

"Have one of these," Anthony teases, dangling a blackened banana in my face. Nasty.

"No, thanks very much," I say, grabbing a container of chocolate milk, a brownie, and a toasted bagel with cheese instead. I figure that as long as I get one or two food groups at lunch, I'm doing okay. I might have to start bringing my lunch from home.

We're headed toward a side table in the main area of the cafeteria when someone grabs my elbow. It's Walt from soccer tryouts last week.

"Congrats, Jeff," Walt says, extending his hand for a shake.

Both of my hands are busy holding my tray, so I grunt in his direction. "Thanks."

"Coach Byrnes thinks you're an ace," Walt goes on. "But you know that already."

"Yeah?" I ask, trying to act super-modest.

"Yeah. All the guys on the team are impressed. Why don't you come over and sit with us?"

I shoot a glance at the table where Walt's pointing. The entire soccer team is sitting there, shoulder to shoulder.

Peter pushes me from behind. "Go ahead," he whispers.

"Nah," I stutter. "What about you guys? We always eat together."

I look back at Anthony. He nods that I should go, too. Then I turn back to Walt.

Maybe I'll try out the soccer table — just this once.

I leave my friends behind and follow Walt to the table. He tells everyone to shove over and I nod hello. Then I sit on the corner edge of the table bench and rip open my milk carton for a slurp.

"That's your lunch?" some beefy-looking kid asks me. I see a plate of the surprise meat loaf on his tray, half-eaten.

He must be an eighth grader. He must be really brave, too, to eat that.

"Um, I'm not that hungry," I explain, severely grossed-out by the black crust on his slab of loaf. *That* must be the surprise part.

The soccer table guys talk about one thing at lunch: soccer. They tell stories about Coach Byrnes and share secrets about crazy things that have happened at Westcott soccer games in the past. They talk about shopping for cleats. They talk about backfield, midfield, and goals. I listen quietly in the corner. In some ways, it's like my dream cafeteria experience, only I don't really have much to add. Not yet, anyway.

"So how do you like Westcott so far?" a seventh grader named Blake asks me. He's skinny and chews his nails.

"It's good," I say. "I hope classes aren't too tough."

"Nah, sixth grade is a breeze," Blake says, still chewing his thumb.

"You played soccer long?" Will asks. I immediately have a flashback to tryouts when Will's sharp kick breezed past my head.

"Since I was a kid," I say, realizing as I say it that I still *am* a kid.

"I want to play in the World Cup one day," Will declares.

"Me, too," I admit sheepishly. All these guys at the table have the exact same fantasy as me. I guess that means I fit in.

"What position do you think Coach Byrnes will start you at?" Walt asks.

I think for a minute. "Maybe fullback?"

Someone further down the table fakes a gasp. "That's Clark's position," he says.

"Yeah," a guy that I can only assume is Clark says, standing up like he's going to get mad all over the place.

"Well, I don't really know what position. . . . I guess whatever Coach thinks . . ." I stammer nervously. The guys are all acting pretty nice to me, but I'm still having trouble figuring out when they're joking and when they're being serious. And I want — no, I *need* — them to like me.

Midway through my first official soccer lunch, I spot Taryn across the cafeteria. She sees me, too. Her hand flies up and she smiles.

I look the other way. What will the soccer guys think if I wave to some girl?

Even though I'm pretending to ignore her, I can still see Taryn out of the corner of my eye. She's *still* waving. A part of me wants to hold up a sign that says HEY, STOP, CAN'T YOU SEE I'M HANGING WITH THE GUYS?

But then there's another part of me that feels this twang of guilt. After all, she is my friend, right? So what's the big deal?

Before I have a chance to do anything else, Taryn walks right up to the soccer table. There's no ignoring her now.

"Hey," she says.

"Hey," I mutter, hoping none of the guys notice. I shoot her a fake smile.

"Didn't you see me?" she asks.

"Where?"

"There," Taryn says, pointing toward the table where she had been sitting.

I hang my head down and stare at my bagel. "Nope, didn't see you," I say. If I have to lie, I can't look right at her while I'm doing it.

"So where were you all weekend?" Taryn asks.

"Around."

"We went up to my aunt's house for an overnight," she says.

"Oh." I'm trying to keep the conversation short and sweet, but she keeps asking all these questions.

"Um . . . why are you sitting over here today?" she asks.

"Soccer," I say, hoping no one else is listening. "The team."

A few seats down, I see Walt staring. What am I supposed to do now? My eyes flicker between Walt, my tray, and Taryn.

Instead of walking away and getting the hint, she crouches down and whispers, "Okay, well. I just wanted to talk to you about going to the bookstore —"

"Wednesday, right?"

"Right." She hands me a slip of paper with the name of the bookstore, the day (Wednesday), the time (five o'clock), and the words FLOYD FANATICS UNITE! written in purple pen. Great.

"Fine," I say, shoving the paper into my pocket. "I'll meet you there."

Taryn steps back just a little. I can see she's getting annoyed. She's on to me.

"You don't have to be a jerk. . . ." Taryn says.

Guys down the other end of the soccer table snicker. Their eyes target me like lasers.

"Jeff," Taryn continues. "I thought you *wanted* to go to the book signing."

I shrug but don't say anything.

"So?" she asks, poking me in the arm.

I still say nothing.

"So . . . I guess I'll talk to you later then," Taryn finally says, exasperated. She turns and heads back to her lunch table with Leslie and Cristina. Of course, they start to whisper the moment Taryn sits down.

Girls.

The soccer guys don't say anything about my little encounter, but I know what they're thinking. Then Walt stands up.

"Let's bail," he says.

"Like a whale," another guy says, flicking Walt's ear.

Just then, the cafeteria bell rings loudly. Class periods are about to start all over again. After the bells, everyone bolts: the team, Peter and Anthony, and even TLC take off. Even though I was still sitting

90

at a table packed with guys a minute ago, I end up standing all by myself.

I walk back toward the nearly deserted kitchen and clear my dirty tray. Then I grab two granola bars, pay, and shove them in my pockets. I'll try to eat them before my math diagnostic test next period. I'm going to need a major dose of brain food if I'm going to test into the right math class. After all, when I get home, Mom is *definitely* going to grill me about everything math-related.

If only I could get graded on my soccer playing.

Then I'd be at the top of the class.

Chapter 9

❀ ❀ ❀ TARYN ❀ ❀ ❀

Four Eyes

It's Tuesday and I'm standing in front of the mirror with my mouth stretched open, about to let out the biggest, loudest screech I can.

Only no noise comes out.

I don't know what to say or how to feel or even what to think right now.

Hello, my name is Taryn Taylor, and I wear glasses.

Mom helped me choose these frames yesterday afternoon. They're not so bad, really: wire-rimmed, copper-colored, with anti-scratch, nonreflective lenses. Since I already had my prescription from Dr. Wexler, we went to one of those places where they have all these display cases packed with

92

frames and where they make new glasses for you in an hour. I thought instant photo places and Pizza Huts were the only places that promised service in such a short period of time. Apparently, that's not true. Eyeglass places fit into that category, too.

I just can't get used to having something on the bridge of my nose like this, no matter how light the frames are. They make my face itch. And why are my eyes magnified to twice their size? That's what I see looking back at me, anyway. Big, dark green saucer eyes. Ugh.

Mom comes into the bathroom to see how I'm doing with my new look. She rubs my shoulders and kisses the top of my head, which makes me feel better for exactly thirty seconds. After that, my nose starts to itch again and I get cold feet about showing my face in public. Even though Mom has been trying to encourage me all morning long (I've been up since 5:46 A.M.), nothing about my glasses seems to look right.

Eventually, I have to race out the front door to catch the school bus. I'm still wearing the glasses, but my head is bent so far over that no one can tell I have them on.

At the bus stop, though, Emma Wallace notices my new look right away.

"Nice glasses," she says as soon as she sees me.

"Thanks," I mumble, staring at the ground. I hope she means it.

"You know, my sister wears glasses to see things that are far away," she goes on. "She likes her tortoiseshell frames, but says glasses always make her nose itch."

"Yeah," I say. "Mine itch, too."

"Those frames go great with your hair and shirt," Emma says, laying on the compliments like buttercream frosting.

Sometimes she's just *too* nice. Why does she have to try so hard?

I look from side to side, scoping the crowd for Jeff. But he's not here yet. I didn't have time to go by his house this morning. Besides, I haven't actually talked to Jeff since yesterday at lunch when he was hanging with his soccer buddies, acting like some kind of VIP. He tried to blow me off. Ha! No one blows off Taryn Taylor. I'll get him back later — for sure.

Hopefully, L and C were wrong when they said that being the youngest kid on the team will give Jeff a big head. I say his head is already plenty big enough.

Emma asks me to sit with her again. But I say "No, thanks," as usual. Instead, I sit in one of the middle rows. As we drive off, staring out of the bus window becomes this totally different experience for me. It's the glasses. All at once, fuzzy trees sharpen so I can see the smooth outline of leaves and jagged bark and squirrels, with their tails flicking across the branches. For once I can actually read street signs and shop signs, and even the cottonball clouds in the sky seem clearer. I can see anything and everything — even a zit on the back of this eighth grader's neck right in front of me.

Blecch.

I look around and notice other kids on the bus who wear glasses like me. There's one kid with big, huge, black frames that dwarf his round face. There's another girl with cat's-eye, pointy-corner glasses, who looks like she's trying too hard to look hip. It's funny how I never really noticed these particular kids before. Now that I have glasses, I can physically *see* my classmates close-up, as opposed to seeing big blurs that just look like middle-schoolers.

So I guess I'm glad to have the glasses. I just need to get the hang of them.

The ride to school seems to take longer than usual today since I don't have Jeff there to keep me company, but I'm really enjoying the view. Soon enough, I'm out of the bus, up the school steps, searching for L and C. I head for my locker near homeroom 10A and wonder if Jeff got a ride to school again today.

"Look at YOU!" Leslie cries as soon as I walk up to the lockers.

"Wow! You look great!" Cristina says.

My cheeks blush. "Thanks," I whisper, grinning.

"You look like a model in those glasses," Leslie gushes. Sometimes she likes to overstate stuff. But I don't mind overstatement this morning — at least not from her. My glasses and I are happy to accept kind words from a best friend. I guess it's just Emma's compliments that bug me.

"Let's get your hair out of that ponytail," Cristina, my fashion advisor, says.

"Not a chance," I snap back.

The tallest kid in sixth grade, Danny Bogart, strolls by and Cristina elbows me in the side. She has sharp elbows.

"What did you do that for?" I moan.

"Did you see Danny? Oh, wow, he's so dreamy. His eyes are dreamy. His shirt is dreamy. Even his freckles are dreamy." Cristina makes these googly eyes and flutters her eyelashes.

"Oh, brother," I say to Leslie. "Cristina's gone nuts."

"Yeah," Leslie says. "No one should get *that* bugged about some boy."

I laugh out loud. "Ha! What about you and Charlie West?" I say to Leslie. "You've got a radar detector for that guy. You just said yesterday that he was cuter than anyone you'd ever met."

"Tarrrrryn," Cristina groans.

"Yeah," Leslie says. "Well, just because you're afraid to admit how much you secretly love Jeff. . . ."

"Stop saying that!" I howl. "That is so not true."

"Oh, come on. You must have a crush on *someone*," Cristina insists. "You just don't want to admit it. Jeff is the obvious choice."

"I don't have a crush, I don't," I reply, rolling my eyes. "Can we change the subject, *please*? Someone might hear."

Right then, I recognize familiar voices, getting closer. Then I spot Jeff, Peter, and Anthony scuffling down the hall in our direction. They walk three-across, shoulder-to-shoulder, stopping next to an orange locker. Anthony breaks formation and opens the locker, reaching for a book. Then Peter leans down to tie his shoe. It's weird, I notice that Jeff's all decked out in a checkered shirt and Levis.

"I can't believe I'm saying this," Cristina says. "But Jeff looks nice."

"No, he doesn't," I scoff, checking him out again.

What's the big deal?

As they're standing there, a cluster of girls passes in the hallway. And who's at the front of the pack? Emma Wallace.

Of course.

I watch as Emma and her friends stop to say hello to the boys. She's standing really close to Jeff and he's grinning nonstop, like some kind of smile robot. He keeps nodding his head up and down, up and down, up and down. Is there someone behind him pulling the strings? I've never seen him act like this. What could he and Emma possibly be talking — and smiling — about? And why do I even care?

"Check her out," Leslie snipes. "See what I mean about Emma's head? It's humongous."

I cross my arms in front. "I know," I say. "She really thinks she's all that, doesn't she?"

"All that and then some," Leslie adds.

"Miss Perfection," Cristina says.

"That is so weird, seeing them flirt with each other," Leslie says.

I think about what she says. My new glasses give me a better look. Is Jeff *flirting*? The whole concept of Jeff and Emma making googly eyes at each other causes my stomach to do flips.

"Obviously Emma likes his outfit," Cristina says.

"So?" I ask.

"So . . ." Leslie jumps in. "You know how that works."

No, I don't. I don't know anything, it seems.

As I'm staring right at the group of them, Jeff looks up. He catches my eye and just like that, he stops talking to Emma and comes over. The boys follow Jeff to where we're standing. Emma and her pals follow, too.

"What's up, Taryn?" Jeff says. Everyone else exchanges hellos.

I wait patiently for Jeff to say something about my glasses.

Does he even notice that I have them on?

Emma is as polite as ever, which totally makes my skin crawl.

Leslie sighs and I can see the look in Cristina's eyes that says, "I am SO out of here."

I'm still waiting for Jeff to say something nice.

Waiting . . .

Waiting . . .

Then he finally clears his throat and grins.

"So . . . how do you like your new glasses, *Four Eyes*?"

There is dead silence. At least there's dead silence inside my head. Jeff looks at me with this dumb smile on his face. Then he looks back at Peter and Anthony. And then everyone, *everyone* except L and C, bursts into laughter.

My knees turn to jelly.

Then Cristina steps right over to Jeff. "I can't believe you said that," she huffs.

Jeff pretends to look stunned by Cristina's angry reaction. But I can tell he still thinks it's funny.

"What's your problem?" Jeff asks.

"You know what the problem is?" Cristina says. "Y-O-U."

"W-H-A-T?" Jeff spells back, like he's trying to be cute or something. This makes Peter and Anthony laugh even harder. But I know what's up. He's just showing off for Emma and everybody else.

Now it's Leslie's turn to get him back.

"L-O-S-E-R," she says, wagging an index finger in his face.

"I know how to spell, *Les*," Jeff grunts.

When he calls her that nickname, Leslie's whole face scrunches up like a geyser ready to burst. Without another word, she and Cristina each take one of my arms and spin me around so we're walking away from Jeff.

"What's the matter, Four Eyes?" Anthony calls out after us.

Peter joins in. "Got a problem, Four Eyes?" he asks.

I can hear Jeff and the other boys laughing — and I want to disappear, right there, right in the middle of the hallway.

Plus, I want to rip my glasses off — NOW.

Jeff always calls me names. He's been making up mean names for me ever since we were little. They have never bugged me. But he's never, EVER called me a name in public, especially not in school. Especially not in front of Emma and other girls like her. And now his friends are calling me the same name, too!

Talk about a nightmare — with a capital *N*.

Jeff knows how hard it was for me to get used to the idea of glasses. He heard me worrying about it all last week. He even said Tim was mean for teasing me about Dr. Wexler. And now *this*?

"Ignore that jerk," Leslie crows as we walk fast.

"He's acting so un-Jeff these days," Cristina says.

"It must be sixth grade, or soccer," Leslie says.

"Yeah," I say, realizing *just* how weird Jeff has been acting since the school year started. Whatever the reason for his attitude, I'm feeling insecure all over again.

"Do you guys think the glasses make me look bad?" I ask my friends. "Be honest."

"No!" Leslie cries. "And if they did, we'd totally tell you."

Dozens of kids race past, searching for their classrooms. We've been back in school a few days now, but there's still a mass of confusion about where, when, and how to get to different places in the building. They should teach a class in figuring out where you're going.

All at once, Cristina stops short. "I have a brilliant idea," she says.

"What?" I ask, hoping that it really is brilliant.

"A makeover!" Cristina declares.

I stare at her. "Huh?"

"That's a great idea!" Leslie says.

"Isn't it?" Cristina says, looking pleased with herself. "We can find a trendy outfit in one of those celebrity magazines and you can raid our closets and wear your hair down for a change —"

"I told you, I don't want to change my hair," I say. My breath feels shallow. I know there are tears in there somewhere. I just don't want them to come out in school. Please don't let them come out in school.

"Why do I need a makeover?" I ask quietly. "It's the glasses, isn't it?"

"No, of course not," Cristina says, putting her arm around me. "The makeover is just to make *you* feel better. Everyone needs a makeover now and then — even *moi*."

"Cristina's right," Leslie says. "We'll show Jeff and Emma and everyone 'Four Eyes.' Ha!"

I cringe when she says the words "Four Eyes," but somehow I'm feeling cheerier. My friends usually do know best. The last time we did anything like this was over the summer. We painted each others' toenails with little palm trees and yellow moons. Cristina stuck on mini-crystals for stars. Everyone at the pool was totally impressed.

"Let's do the makeover next week, right before the carnival," Leslie says.

"Awesome!" Cristina says. "That way you'll look like a princess the next day."

"Maybe," I mutter, feeling slightly self-conscious. "I just need to check with my mom."

"Let's do it Thursday, right after school. I can throw some ideas together before then," Cristina says, slipping into full fashion-advisor mode.

At once, the class bell rings. Now we have to hurry. In a flash, Cristina's already halfway down the hall.

"Taryn, wait," Leslie says, taking my arm before I dash off, too. "Just because we want to give you a makeover doesn't mean you aren't beautiful already. Because you are. You know that, right?"

I look at Leslie's yellow-blond hair, cute Hello Kitty! T-shirt; and fitted-at-the-waist, flared-at-the-cuff white pants. I guess she must know what she's talking about. After all, *she's* beautiful. What else can I say?

"Right," I reply.

Leslie looks happy to hear my positive response. As we walk on, I catch my reflection in the window of a science lab room. I wonder what I would look like without the ponytail.

For the first time, I consider the possibility that maybe change doesn't have to be so scary or awful like I've always thought. Maybe it's like Mom's far-out dinners.

A little octopus or rutabaga never *really* hurt anyone. Right?

Chapter 10

••• Jeff •••

Miss Understanding

I haven't seen Taryn since this morning in the hall. I know she's avoiding me. It's the whole Four Eyes thing. L and C act like some kind of army of two, protecting Taryn from the enemy who is so obviously me. Why can't everyone just lighten up? Okay, so I shouldn't have called T that name, but somehow it just slipped out.

The glasses didn't even look that bad.

I have to stop thinking about this. First of all, I've got a full day of classes. I only skim-read my first English assignment and my new science teacher gives me the creeps. Then we have soccer practice today after school and I need to be in A-plus form. All eyes are on the new kid, after all.

That's what Walt and Will tell me. There's a scrimmage tomorrow and scrimmages count.

The team meets up in the locker room after school to change. Then we jog over to the field together. When we get there, Coach Byrnes gives us a pre-season pep talk. He carries around this clipboard and whistle and talks really, really fast.

"Passtheballovertherenowturnaroundandkick-itintothegoalrightnow!"

Sometimes I have no idea what he's talking about. I thought I knew everything there was to know about soccer. Boy, was I wrong.

The sky is gray and overcast. I'm on my back with the rest of the team, doing sit-ups, staring at the thick clouds. I can hear all the guys around me huffing and puffing as they do their warm-ups. It doesn't take me long to make friends with this one seventh grader named Jake. I remember him from tryouts and lunch the other day, and he's a total crack-up. We compare notes about games and practical jokes. I realize he's the only other person I've ever met who actually ate rocks on a dare, just like me. Together, we hatch an instant plot to apply to one of those reality shows like *Fear Factor*. We'd be an awesome team.

Just before practice, Jake told me what it was like to be one of the lucky sixth-grade soccer recruits *last* year. He tells me that I shouldn't get my hopes up too high about playing in a real game.

"Coach'll keep you on the bench mostly," Jake says. "But you can't bum out, no matter what."

"I won't," I say, laughing it off.

Bench? Ha! We'll see about that.

Of course, a half hour later, I'm beginning to believe what Jake says. Coach Byrnes benches me and doesn't even assign me a real position. I have no idea where I'm slotted on the team, so I watch the other guys kicking the ball around and pick at a scab on my knee.

Some of these guys aren't that great, but some are amazing. Walt jumps way off the ground and heads the ball into the goal. I wish I had a chance to get out there and prove my stuff, too. Lots of people come to watch our practices and scrimmages, and I want to show them all what I'm made of.

There are only ten minutes left of "official" practice when Coach finally calls me and a few of the other benched guys onto the field. We all look at each other, eager to have a chance to shine. When the soccer ball finally drifts my way, I dribble it all the way down the field, only to have it kicked away by a mysterious cleat. I'm so focused on the ball that I don't even see the foot coming.

The whistle blows and practice ends. I feel like a flat tire, but Jake tells me not to worry so much. Then we hustle back to the locker room.

Once we're all changed, the team splits up and heads home. I grab my backpack and head into the school hallway. I'm thinking that maybe I can still catch Taryn when she gets out of her carnival planning meeting.

Yeah, I owe her.

I casually walk up to the door of 12C where the meetings are usually held, only the room is empty. There's no sign on the door, either. No alternate location. Maybe I should scout around the rest of the floor? Put out an all-points bulletin?

Nah, I don't have time. And the more I think about it, the more I realize that I am a little afraid to see T in person right now. Maybe a note is better? I tear off the corner of a page from my math notebook and start to write.

Dear T — I looked 4 u but ur gone. Sorry about what happened &
I really shouldn't have said that. Hey, I'd be SOO psyched if u came
2 my soccer scrimmage Wed. (2morrow). It's field B as always,
right after school gets out. C U THERE! Don't 4get. Bye, J

When I'm done writing, I fold the note into quarters and slide it into the slat of Taryn's locker.

Hopefully the paper won't fall out.

Hopefully she'll be Miss Understanding.

Hopefully, she'll accept my apology *and* my invitation to come to soccer. I could really use the moral support. If I even get to play, that is.

There are lots of kids still milling around outside the school. I notice Taryn's pal Cristina, standing with a whole bunch of girls dressed in white shorts. I forgot she plays tennis. I give Cristina a wave but she ignores me — big-time — even though I know for a fact that she saw me. I guess I deserve it.

Everyone else is standing around waiting for their parents or somebody to pick them up. It's like a middle school people jam out here. There's a long line of cars in the cul-de-sac, too. I never saw so many minivans in one place.

Finally, I spot Peter sitting on a low wall next to the school. He waves me over. We walk a block or two to the local park. Anthony is waiting there with his bike. He's already been home and back again.

We play catch for about a half hour. Then Anthony takes off on his bike. He needs to get home to walk his dog. Peter has to split, too. He has relatives coming in from out of town and his mom's making a Greek feast. That just reminds me how hungry I am.

Peter flips open his cell phone to call his sister, Marisa. All the way home in Marisa's huge boat of a car, Peter won't shut up. He and Marisa fight over the CD player. I get a little nervous when he wrestles her arm off the remote. After all, she *is* driving.

Meanwhile, way, way, *way* back in the big backseat, I'm dreaming of spaghetti. That's what's on the table every Tuesday at the Rasmussen house, and I'm starved.

If I can't count on playing first string on the soccer team, and I can't count on Taryn giving me a break, at least there are some things I can count on these days.

Even if they are just garlic bread and meatballs.

Chapter 11

❀ ❀ ❀ TARYN ❀ ❀ ❀

Talking Boycott

I woke up this morning and decided that maybe I really *do* need a makeover.

I also decided that Jeff is, categorically, a big fat jerk. Those are really Leslie and Cristina's words, but I agree with them.

After all, best friends know best, don't they?

Here's my plan: I am executing a talking boycott today, at least as far as Jeff is concerned. Maybe this will get him to apologize for what he said and how he's been acting these past few days. A little cold shoulder will definitely freeze that boy out.

At least I hope it will. Sometimes it's hard to follow through on these things.

The bus ride to school is Test One. Jeff is at the

bus stop for the first time in a couple of days, and he's joking around with some other guys. Emma's there, too, standing near them and smiling.

I merge into the crowd of kids, decked out in my embroidered jean jacket, purple cotton pants, and lace-up flats. Cristina called me last night to help pick my outfit over the telephone, so I'm feeling fashion friendly this morning.

I haven't been standing there for more than a blink when Jeff sees me and waves.

My stomach grinds. I don't acknowledge him, even though it's way harder to ignore my former best friend than I thought it would be.

Jeff waves again, but when I don't respond a second time, he gives up.

He doesn't even walk over to me.

That's weird.

The bus driver opens the squeaky bus door and we all pile inside. I wait until the very last minute to climb on. The middle rows, where I've been sitting happily for the past few days, are full, so I squeeze into the front part of the bus.

"Hey, aren't you on the carnival committee?" some boy asks. He's wearing glasses just like me, but I don't recognize him from sixth-grade home-room or anywhere else at Westcott so far.

"Yeah, I am," I say.

"I thought I remembered you from the meeting last week," he says. "I'm Alex."

"I'm Taryn."

"Are you in sixth grade?"

"Yeah, are you?"

He shakes his head. "Nah, I'm in seventh."

The bus is getting noisier by the second, so I can hardly hear myself think, let alone hear what Alex is saying to me. I wonder why I've never noticed him before now.

He leans a little closer to the edge of his seat and I can hear him better. "I was on the carnival committee last year," he says. "Mr. Wood is the best."

"He seemed kind of . . . well . . . nervous at first," I stammer, sounding kind of nervous myself, although I have no idea why.

"He sweats a lot," Alex says plainly. "But the truth is: He keeps his cool. Trust me. Carnival is one of the best experiences I've had at Westcott. Last year, the money we made helped to pay for the new climbing wall in the gym. This year, they're trying to add a special multimedia area in the library. And most of the other money is given to charity."

"Those are all the reasons I signed up," I explain.

"Me, too."

"So what else do you do at school?" I ask.

"Chess club, math Olympiad, and debate."

"Oh," I say, and the word "brainiac" pops into my head.

In no time, we pull into the school parking lot. I get off the bus first, and Alex follows right behind me. A few seconds later, I hear my name. It's not L or C calling me.

It's Jeff.

"Wait up, Taryn!" Jeff hollers. I pause and think about turning around, breaking my boycott, and saying good morning. But then I decide to keep right on walking. Alex is talking to me the whole time. He's the perfect alibi.

There are so many kids squeezing inside the school doors that Jeff can't catch up to me. Once we're inside, Alex dashes off to his homeroom. I'll see him later at the carnival meeting.

When I reach my locker, I dial the combination and stuff my bag inside. It's only been a week of school and already my small locker is crammed with a pair of shoes, books, and some random paper scraps. I can't deal with any of it right now, I think as I push everything to the back and click the lock. Maybe I'll clean it out later.

Across the hall, through the crowd, I see Leslie

and Cristina at their lockers, too. I approach them quickly with the 4-1-1 on the Jeff situation.

My friends don't look surprised by my talking boycott; in fact, Cristina gives me a cheer for the whole plan. They don't mind my complaining a little more than usual about Jeff this morning, either. In no time, the conversation has shifted from chatting about our weekends to boy talk. L and C pipe up about their latest Charlie West and Danny Bogart sightings. For a split second, I think about mentioning Alex from the bus. After all, he's a boy, and Leslie told me she wants to be informed of any boy–girl contact I may have. But she's so insistent about the fact that I have a secret crush that I don't want her to get the wrong idea and think that crush is *Alex*.

So I keep my lips zipped.

We all slip into Homeroom 10A just as the bell rings.

During my first two classes, reading and math, I don't see any sign of Jeff. By third period, social studies, I run into him in the hallway. He's bound and determined to stop me in my tracks.

"Taryn," Jeff says, putting his hand out to stop me.

"Jeff," I snap, biting my tongue. So much for the talking boycott.

"I've been looking for you, T. What's your problem? Didn't you hear me call you this morning at the bus stop? And before homeroom?"

"Um . . . no," I say with a shrug.

"Well, I saw you," Jeff says emphatically. "And I thought you saw me."

"You mean like how I thought I saw you in the cafeteria the other day?" I ask.

"Uhh . . . not exactly . . ."

Jeff rocks from foot to foot. A quiet moment passes. We're still standing there in the hallway not saying much.

"Okay then, if that's it," I say, breaking the silence first, "I have to go."

"Go where?"

"To social studies. Duh. Don't you have class?"

"Yeah, but what about later today? I'm going to see you, right? After school, I mean. We have a plan."

"A plan?" I repeat.

My head spins. Of course! I'd almost forgotten. Later today is the book signing with our favorite author in the whole wide world, Floyd Flannigan. With all of the angry back and forth between Jeff and I over the past few days, it nearly slipped my mind. But Jeff remembered?

"We do have a plan," I say to him with a small smile.

"Cool," Jeff says. "So I'll see you there?"

"Yeah, I'll see you there," I reply. "Unless you see me first. Ha, ha."

Jeff chuckles at my lame joke attempt. It feels — for a second — like everything is back to normal between us. Then we walk off in opposite directions. I have Social Studies this period and we're getting another textbook.

As the day goes on, I begin to feel better and better about Jeff and the fact that I didn't have to cut off all conversation for the entire day. Tonight, when we Floyd Fanatics unite, everything will be patched up for good.

But L and C still think I should be giving Jeff the silent treatment.

"Are you saying that Jeff still hasn't apologized for the whole Four-Eyes thing?" Leslie asks me at the end of the school day. "Like, he didn't say those exact words, 'I'm sorry?'"

"Not exactly," I reply.

"And after everything that happened, you're still going to the book signing with him?" Cristina asks.

I nod. "What's the big deal?"

"Taryn!" Leslie snaps. "*You're* the big deal. He owes you a real apology."

"You guys don't understand. I know Jeff. He's been my best friend since forever. He's probably just waiting to apologize until later when we're at the bookstore. I know he'll do the right thing."

"Yeah, sure," Cristina says, looking in the opposite direction.

I'm not sure what to say now. Maybe friends don't always know best about some things.

Like the boy next door.

After classes end for the day, my life becomes a little bit of a drag race. I take the steps two at a time up to the carnival meeting. The room is packed. As soon as I spot Alex near the windowsill with an open seat next to him, I sit nearer to the door. For some reason, I don't feel like talking to him right now. I have another boy on my mind.

Mr. Wood passes out more lists of things to do. He hands me a bright yellow team leader folder, and I am floored. On top it reads: TARYN TAYLOR, TEAM LEADER in all capital letters. That makes me sound so important.

Across the room, Alex holds up a two-finger-split sign for peace. Or is it some kind of Star Trek code? I'm not sure. I wonder what Jeff would think of him. I *know* what L and C would think.

Inside the folder, I find all sorts of papers about how to organize and play the different carnival games like Bottle Toss, Cake Walk, and Wheel of Fortune. A small group of us talk about how we'll organize materials for those games, and who will man the booths once everything has been set up. I take a bunch of notes. Mr. Wood tells me that the difference between a regular Carnival volunteer and a team leader is simple: INITIATIVE. To be honest, I had to look up that word. But now I know it means being the *first* one to get to the meetings, to collect information, and to get everyone pumped up.

Today's meeting lasts exactly fifty minutes. I'm amazed that when I share my ideas and notes kids listen to me. Me! Even with all the work I do, I'm out the door before four, just in time to catch the late bus that makes stops in our neighborhood. For some reason, Alex isn't right behind me so he misses the bus.

Whew. No distractions.

After a bumpy bus ride home, I walk inside the door of our house. Right away my brother Tom gives me grief about driving me to the bookstore signing. I had said he could drop me off at four-thirty, but now it's four thirty-eight and he says, "I really have somewhere *else* to go."

Tom and I yell at each other for exactly two minutes. This makes Mom crazy. She throws her hands into the air and Tom stomps out of the room — just like that. Exasperated, Mom volunteers to drive me to the bookstore herself.

"I'm really sorry," I tell Mom later as the two of us climb into the car.

"That brother of yours . . ." Mom says, gritting her teeth. "But this works out better. I was curious about this book signing. You've been reading those outer space books for a long time, haven't you?"

Mom quickly shifts the car into gear and drives downtown. I stare out the window as we go, pressing my nose to the pane, only my glasses get in the way and I bonk my forehead.

I'm still having trouble getting used to these things. At least they don't look so terrible.

When we arrive at the bookstore, I'm glad to have Mom along for company. There's a long line already forming inside the store by the signing area, and I can see signs with Floyd Flannigan's photograph. The oversized author picture is the same one that's on the flap of all his book covers. In the photo, he's dressed in some kind of tweed jacket and tie. His face has all the nooks and crannies of an English muffin. He has a long, unkempt gray beard, a crooked grin, and squinty eyes that look like they've been glued shut. He's my hero.

I scan the room for Jeff's baseball cap while Mom takes a place in line. They're handing out numbers, so everyone who gets one is guaranteed a signed copy of his latest title in the Outer Space Chronicles, "Madman from Mars: Return of the One-Armed Alien."

As I move around the bookstore from one pack of fans to the next, my pulse quickens. It's one of those moments when everything comes together in just the right way. I can't wait to talk to Jeff. He's the only person I know who understands just what it means to be a true Floyd Fanatic.

This is a once-in-a-lifetime moment, for sure.

Mom gets our numbers (49, 50, and 51) and manages to find two folding chairs where we can watch the reading part of the event. By now, it's a little bit after five o'clock. Jeff isn't here yet. Luckily, neither is Floyd. There's still time.

By quarter after five, Mom actually looks a little worried about Jeff's no-show.

"Should we call his house?" she asks me.

"Not yet," I say, stalling. "He's just late."

I stand up and search the crowd again, but it's no use. Jeff isn't in there. And for the first time, I begin to suspect that he isn't coming.

Someone behind me starts to clap and then the whole room bursts into applause. I see Floyd Flannigan enter the room. He's at least six feet tall, way taller than the bookstore employees who escort him to the front of the room. I clap along with everyone else. Then Mom leans into me again.

"Taryn," she whispers. "Maybe Jeff just forgot. There's still time for him to get here. Let me call . . ."

Unfortunately, by the time Mom begins to dial Jeff's house, a clerk tells her to turn off her cell phone. The reading begins and everyone has to hush up.

Floyd starts to read the first chapter of his latest saga in his thick brogue. I feel quite speechless myself, and not in a good way. As exciting as all of this is, the signing just doesn't feel the same without Jeff.

I close my eyes and try to focus on Floyd's words to block out my surging feelings of disappointment.

But it's no use.

Somehow, I fear that there's a *second* talking boycott in my cards.

Starting. Right. Now.

Chapter 12

••• JeFF •••

Pants on Fire

So I'm lying in bed after my alarm clock goes off this morning, Thursday, staring at the piles on my shelves. My eyes move across the room, and I see all this stuff I know I don't need but can't (or won't) throw out. But I know the time to toss is coming fast. I reached critical mass a long time ago.

J.D. told me that we're having a yard sale. He's already picked a good weekend next month to do it. Meanwhile, Mom just wants to give everything away. I can just see her heaving my clothes and books into one of those enormous black trash bags. She'll cart it over to the Salvation Army faster than

I can say, "Hold up, I really need my second-grade Transformers lunch box!"

Okay, I admit there's a lot up there: maybe two hundred Matchbox cars, shoeboxes of baseball and Yu-Gi-Oh trading cards, a stuffed alligator with the eyes chewed off (I've had that since I was born), marbles, and way too many books to count. In fact, I have an entire shelf devoted to my favorite author, Floyd Flannigan.

Gulp.

That's when it hits me.

I forgot about the book signing.

I leap up from my bed and race over to a wall calendar tacked on the door. Is the bookstore signing today? Tomorrow? Then I remember the piece of crumpled paper in the pocket of my jeans. Taryn handed me that note at lunch the other day. I'd forgotten all about it — and the signing — until just now.

I fish through the pile of dirty laundry on my closet floor. The jeans in question are right there. And there, too, in the right pocket, along with a chipped Wint-O-Green Life-Saver, is one crumpled slip of paper with the name of the bookstore and time. The words, FLOYD FANATICS UNITE are written in capital letters alongside, WEDNESDAY.

Oh, no. That was yesterday.

My stomach lurches. I definitely missed the signing.

I collapse back onto my bed, rubbing my eyes hard. I can't believe I missed it.

How did things get so messed up?

My first instinct is to call Taryn, of course. But it's too early. She's probably in the shower or eating breakfast. I'll see her later on the bus. I can explain then.

I just can't believe it. There I was yesterday, kicking the ball around the soccer field in our very first scrimmage, looking for encouragement. All I've been able to think about for the past week or so has been soccer. Of course, my sister, Blair, would say that all I *ever* think about is soccer. But who listens to her — except for poor Toots? And he doesn't have much of a choice.

Yesterday, I wondered why Taryn didn't show up at my scrimmage. I wanted her to see me play, but then she wasn't in the stands. We had talked about it, too. When I saw her in the hallway, Taryn told me she would be there. She said those exact words. "See you there." I said them, too. But her "there" and my "there" were two different places!

Peter and Anthony told me she was a bad friend to be a no-show. And I believed them. Does that make me the lamest friend in the history of the universe?

A half hour later, the digital clock reads 7:33 and I contemplate dialing the Taylor house. But still, I don't. I can't see Taryn in her room. So I convince myself that she's busy and can't talk. I think I'm probably just freaked out about what she'll say if I call.

Instead, I pull on my khakis, a blue-striped polo shirt, navy-blue sweatshirt, and my sneakers. Then I run a wet comb through my hair. I have this cowlick that pokes up sometimes in the morning. It's like someone's playing a bad trick on my hair. Today, no matter how hard I try to keep it down, the hair stays poked up.

I yank on a baseball cap, hoping that will help.

After a fast bowl of Honey-Nut O's, I'm off to the bus stop. I cross my fingers and hope to see Taryn leave her house at the same time as me. I have to talk to her, to explain — even if I don't want to. Outside, I pause and wait for nearly five minutes in front of her fence. Wait and hope.

But she's left already. No one comes out. She's gone.

Quickly, I hustle toward the bus stop. There are fewer people than usual but I see all of the regulars, including Emma Wallace. She says hello.

Every day when she does that, Anthony says how much she likes me. That cracks me up. Everyone knows that Emma is just being nice. She does *not* like me.

Taryn never shows up at the bus stop.

Where is she?

I don't say much to my buddies on the ride to school. Peter's blabbing in my face the whole time. Still, I say nada.

When we finally get to Westcott, a few guys from the soccer team are hanging out outside the main school doors. Walt holds up his hand as I walk toward them.

"Good scrimmage yesterday," Walt says. "Coach might put you in a real game now."

"Thanks," I respond. But for the first time since school began, my mind is anywhere *but* soccer. I just want to find Taryn and tell her I'm sorry.

It isn't until the hallway at lunchtime that I see Taryn face-to-face.

Her face is red.

I know I'm in for it.

"Taryn," I say, going close to talk. I try to keep my voice at a whisper so no one around us hears.

"I'm not talking to you," she snaps. But I know she will. She always does.

In the hallway outside the cafeteria, kids stream by. No one seems to pay much attention. I like it that way.

"We need to talk," I say.

"I waited for you," Taryn replies in a low voice.

"The bookstore. I know. I forgot. I swear! I feel terrible, T."

"How could you forget something so important?" she asks.

"Soccer," I say. It sounds lame. But it's the truth.

"It's *always* soccer," Taryn says.

"Was the signing good?" I ask, trying to hit a positive note.

Taryn shoots me a hard look. "Uh-huh. You missed the best-ever book signing ever in the history of book signings. So there."

She has me feeling like I'm only an inch tall by now.

"Taryn," I continue to plead my case. "Why didn't you remind me? Didn't you get my note about the scrimmage?"

"Your note? What note?" Taryn snaps.

"The one I left in your locker."

"You did not leave me a note."

"Yes, I did."

"No, you didn't."

"Yes, I did."

"Liar."

"Whoa." I cough, surprised. She's called me names before, but never anything that mean.

"Pants on fire," Taryn adds, for emphasis.

"I swear. I left you a note the other day. It said I was sorry."

"For what?" Taryn snarls.

"For what I said."

"You mean the whole Four Eyes thing?" Taryn asks pointedly.

I'm glad she said those words and not me.

Now what?

I wait for Taryn to accept my late apology, give me one of her pokes in the shoulder, and tell me to buzz off in that fun way that she does. That would be the happy sitcom ending. But I'm in for a big surprise.

"You know what, Jeff? It's too late to say sorry. First you embarrassed me in front of all those people. Then I waited for you at the bookstore forever. You blew me off and I'm mad at you, and I'm not just going to stop being mad at you for no reason."

"What? No reason? Wait a minute. . . ."

Slowly, over the course of this conversation, our voices have gotten a teeny bit louder. Now I realize we've attracted the attention of some kids and a hall monitor.

This is not a good thing.

"Um . . . can we just start over?" I ask very quietly, trying to lighten up the situation.

"I don't THINK so," Taryn declares in a big voice.

What a drama queen.

"This is stupid," I say. "Don't be stupid, Taryn."

"Now you're telling me I'm stupid?" Taryn exclaims.

"No, that's not what I —"

"*You're* stupid, Jeff Rasmussen. And you're obviously not my friend!"

"Hey! What did you say that for?"

"Because you've been acting weirder and weirder these last few weeks, but especially weird toward me. I thought I knew you better than that. I really and truly thought we were best friends."

"We were." I shrug. "I mean, we *are*."

"Liar."

We stand there, eye to eye and toe to toe. This is the biggest fight we've ever had, by a long shot. I can't believe we're having it at school. We're minutes away from getting reeled in by some teacher passing by.

And I'm not sure what else to say that won't make Taryn madder than an electric eel.

I decide the best thing to do is just walk away.

Taryn calls out after me, but I am so out of there. I'd do anything for a soccer ball right about now. I could kick away all my frustration. Hard.

I head toward the other cafeteria entrance. But first I glance back to see if Taryn's still there.

She is. And she's staring.

By now L and C are there, too, staring just as hard.

And I *really* feel like road kill.

There has to be some way to fix this. I just wish I knew what it was.

Chapter 13

❀ ❀ ❀ TARYN ❀ ❀ ❀

Carnival Shmarnival

Mom made one of her one-of-a-kind, experimental feasts on Sunday.

I have never eaten so much food in my life. I tried everything Mom put in front of me, including these strange, international dishes like Cornish hen with pomegranate sauce, sautéed Swiss chard, and French profiteroles for dessert. Everything was yummy, especially the little vanilla ice-cream puffs with chocolate sauce. Lucky for me, there was no shrimp toast on this menu.

"It's hard to bounce back from a big friend fight," Mom kept telling me.

I know she's right.

When Jeff and I had our big blowout last

Thursday, I thought the universe folded in on itself. I've been thinking a lot about how Jeff and I used to play those secret-agent games. All weekend, I wished for super-binoculars to spy on his every move. I feel like I need to gather evidence and try to figure out why we aren't friends anymore.

Why didn't I see all this coming?

Now that it's Monday, chances are at least fifty-fifty that I'll see Jeff on the bus ride to school this morning. But what am I supposed to say when I see him? Maybe I need to apologize, too? Leslie and Cristina say no way. But I wonder if maybe I over-reacted just a little bit. Mom's always telling me to cut the dramatics. Should I have called, "Cut!" on Thursday or Friday? Should I have left *him* a note?

No, that's how half this mess got started — his stupid note. When I finally pulled it out of the bottom of my locker, I understood our miscommunication, but it didn't make the hurt feelings go away. It was too late for that.

The one I really feel bad for in all this is Zsa-Zsa. My poor kitty has been listening to me talk about Jeff nonstop. The way she mews at me sometimes makes me feel like she understands every word. I don't know what I'd do without her. She purrs and rubs herself against my leg and lets me scratch between her ears and I know everything will be just fine.

Isn't that what a friend is supposed to do, too? Well, except for the purring and rubbing and scratching part, of course.

As early morning passes and it gets closer and closer to the start of the school day, I get cold feet. I'm second-guessing the whole meet-Jeff-on-the-bus thing. Instead, I beg Mom to drive me to school.

The ride over to Westcott turns out to be just what the doctor ordered. I just sit there and Mom drives. We don't even try to have a conversation. I'm so glad she isn't bugging me about Jeff. Not now.

Mom pulls into the school parking lot, and right away I see L and C on the steps. I hug Mom good-bye, hop out of the car, and make a beeline for my two pals.

Cristina has this horrified look on her face.

"Taryn! What are you wearing?" she asks.

"Clothes," I say meekly.

"Taryn, have you let all this Jeff stuff affect your fashion sense? Why didn't you call me this weekend for advice?" Cristina asks. Right now she sounds like one of those obnoxious, know-it-all makeover experts I always see on cable TV.

"I don't need you to pick out my clothes every day, do I?" I ask back, although when I look down at my outfit, I realize she may have a point. Today I'm wearing baggy, striped pants and a flowered shirt with boots and a pilly old sweater that my grandmother sent me about five years ago. The sleeves are a little short. Okay, the sleeves are more than a little short. They go up to my elbows. It's like something I probably shouldn't have worn after second grade.

"Don't forget. Thursday, after school, at my house," Cristina announces as we enter Westcott. "I'm turning my room into makeover central."

Leslie leans in close to me. "It'll be so much fun," she promises in that sweet voice she always uses to make me feel better.

I'm still not one hundred percent convinced. I have a lot on my mind.

"I'm not sure I can do Thursday," I protest. "I may have to do last-minute carnival work that day and there's just so much —"

"Carnival shmarnival," Cristina says. "We made a date."

"Cristina is right." Leslie smiles.

"Okay, okay," I concede. "You win. I'll do it."

"You won't be sorry," Cristina squeals. "I promise."

All week long, thoughts of my pending make-over hang in the back of my mind. But I turn most of my daily attention to one thing: the carnival. All over school, bright posters scream BEACH PARTY! with enormous, orange suns and sailboats dancing in the background. It's like getting the best parts of summer back again.

There are a million and one things to do before Friday comes. Thankfully, my carnival volunteer team is in great shape. As carnival leader, it's my job to keep everyone motivated. All week long we work together after school to paint waves, sandcastles, and seagulls on homemade signs and backdrops. We invented this quicksand pit stop for the beach obstacle course, which is really just a plastic kiddie pool filled with those Styrofoam packing peanuts, but everyone says it's the best. I can't wait to see the kids and teachers trying to wade through that. On our "Wheel of For-tune" game spinner, we added funny categories like "Feeling Crabby," "Something's Fishy," and "Catch the Wave." I think they're a little cheesy, but Mr. Wood loves those sayings.

The volunteers aren't the only ones with carni-val fever. Everyone else in school has it, too. The swim team instructors added a last-minute kickboard and diving contest in the school pool. The newspaper staff decided to issue a special Friday edition of the school paper with the headline, BEACHED! And most teachers volunteered time in the dunk tank. Even Principal Simms is jumping on the bandwagon. Every day during morning announcements he has the school secretary play "Surf City" and "Beach Baby" beach tunes over the loudspeaker. Someone says Principal Simms is planning to show up to the carnival in swim trunks. Ha! People would pay to see that, I bet. Plus, he decided to formally dismiss school for a half day on Friday. That way, everyone can enjoy the carnival before the weekend.

If all this isn't reason to celebrate, then what is?

By late Thursday afternoon, everything is ready to go. During our last meeting, a very sweaty Mr. Wood runs around checking displays and games. Then he gathers us together for a final pep talk, hands us each a name tag, and offers a huge round of applause for all our hard work.

"Let's face it, kids. This is the best beach party I've ever seen," he tells us, clapping all the while. "I can practically smell the suntan lotion."

I'm standing right next to Valerie. She flips her hair and looks right at me with those eyes.

"Didn't I tell you? Isn't this the best of the best?" Val asks.

"You said that," I reply. Somehow, when I'm around Val, I get a little tongue-tied. But Val doesn't seem to notice, or care.

"I can tell Mr. Wood likes you," Val says, smiling.

She starts to say some other nice things, too, but then I realize I'm not really listening to the words. I'm just staring at her hair. Val's long, whirly curls fall perfectly onto her shoulders. In that moment, I want to be *just* like her — hair and all.

Then it dawns on me: My hair *can* look the same. It's Thursday afternoon and my makeover is today! In fact, Leslie and Cristina are waiting for me in the school lobby right now.

As soon as Mr. Wood dismisses us, I gather up my team of carnival volunteers to make sure that everyone knows where and when to meet tomorrow. Then my feet can't carry me to the lobby fast enough. I'm bursting with excitement. L and C look even more excited than me. We head over to Cristina's house, which is only a ten-minute walk away — tops.

Since the last time I visited her house, Cristina painted her bedroom lavender and put up framed posters all over her walls. Her walk-in closet is concealed by these cool curtains that she pulls back so I can see her entire wardrobe. The place looks like something I'd see in a magazine, with brightly colored bean-bag chairs, a rainbow lamp, and shelves of books and magazines.

I wish my room looked like this. Zsa-Zsa would love to nap on a bean bag.

Once we get comfortable, Cristina turns up the radio and tosses a pile of magazines in front of me.

"What do you want to look like?" she asks.

The three of us pore over the pages together, picking out our favorite hairstyles. I find one pic I love of a fancy updo held in place with sparkly clips. But I think L and C have something different in mind.

I'm a size smaller than Cristina, so when she and Leslie hand me clothes to try on, nothing fits quite right. We decide to stick with makeup and hair — as if I've ever used any makeup before now. The only thing I use is lip gloss and I have *that* in about ten different flavors. My favorite is banana split. Jeff made fun of me once for wearing it. He said I smelled like a fruit bowl.

But I am *not* going to think about Jeff right now.

Cristina applies mascara and eye shadow to my eyes and it's all I can do not to wiggle or sneeze.

Then she powders my forehead and dusts blush on my cheeks.

"Not too much," I warn her, worried that I'll come out looking like I've been over-painted.

Cristina grins. "I know, I know," she says. "We're just experimenting. You can redo it yourself in the morning."

"This is SO exciting," Leslie coos, rubbing her hands together.

I want to be excited, too, but not until I see results.

It's nearly six o'clock when Leslie finally hands me a mirror to show me the major makeover. I can't believe how different my face looks with makeup on it, although Cristina overdid it just a little. But I don't have to use all this purple eye shadow when I put it on myself.

My hair, on the other hand, is perfect. I don't even recognize myself. And it's not piled on top of my head — not by a long shot. My brown hair cascades down onto my shoulders, loose and free, just like Valerie's hair. I think it looks even more perfect than Emma's hair, which is saying a lot. I always thought wearing my hair down was flat, straight, and *boring*, but this is something else. And Leslie stuck in these fabulous glitter bobby-pins. . . .

I looooove it.

Dad picks me up in time for dinner and on the ride home, he keeps asking me, "What's different about you tonight, kiddo?"

I just sit there, beaming, with my new 'do and my painted fingernails and funky eyeglasses. "Oh, nothing much," I say with a big grin on my face. Then he realizes what he missed: My hair is different and my cheeks are pinker.

"You must be the prettiest girl in sixth grade," Dad says, winking. "I bet all the boys will notice."

For some reason, this makes me think of Jeff. I've been so focused on beach umbrellas this week that I've forgotten all about boys.

And I can't decide if I'm still mad at Jeff or not.

After nearly five days of my ducking under stairs, hiding behind lockers, and flat-out walking away, Jeff still has yet to say *anything* to me about what's happened. But when he sees me, when he sees *this*, he'll be the one apologizing.

He'd better.

By the time Friday morning rolls around, I'm still in makeover-mode. Last night, Cristina IM-ed me a list of possible outfits and I picked out the things I liked best: my patchwork jean skirt; a blue, scoop-neck T-shirt with a butterfly design on the front; and a cute, comfy pair of purple sneakers. The new ensemble and the new hair put me in a super mood for the carnival. Mom even offers me a ride this morning. I gladly take her up on it.

Let the games begin.

As soon as Cristina and Leslie see me walk up to the school doors, they let out a little cheer. They're happy to see my hair in the same style from the night before. I've put on a little bit of makeup, too, but not so much. Mom wasn't too happy to see me putting on eye shadow this morning. She's okay with lip gloss, and that's about it.

Some kids in my classes notice my new look, but no one says much. Everyone's way too focused on the carnival.

After morning classes, I follow my nose down to the recreation room. The cotton-candy machine is up and running. That was Mr. Wood's brilliant idea. The school rented food machines to feed the hungry masses: cotton candy, popcorn, and even a hot dog rotisserie. I secretly wonder if Mr. Wood rented them for the crowd or just because he loves to snack.

The carnival is supposed to start at one o'clock, just after lunch. It runs during afternoon class time and after school. Right now, it's noon and almost everyone I know is still in the cafeteria eating lunch, including the eight people on my volunteer list.

I've reminded my team about the time to meet. I even left notes in everyone's lockers. But by 12:40, only two of those people have shown up at their booths.

Where is everyone else?

Five minutes pass and another three kids stroll in. But I still have no one to run the bottle toss and I can feel my neck prickle, like I'm getting nervous hives. What's going on? Plus, I'm missing half of the team that mans the great big Wheel of Fortune, a spin-your-luck game with prizes.

I'm down three whole people?

The carnival doors are about to open wide, and I have to face facts: I'm in big trouble. My stomach clenches right along with both of my fists. How could this have happened? I planned so carefully. Everyone was so excited. I can't believe my team flaked, after all our hard work. I glance around. All of the other team leaders seem to be doing fine. Their games are up and running.

I feel tears well up in my eyes. It figures. The first time I attempt to wear mascara, I get all weepy. Wait. Team leaders can't cry. They need to be strong. I think of Val.

Don't cry. Don't cry.

Then I search the room for a faculty advisor who can help me out. Where is Mr. Wood and his sausage arms? Where are the parent advisors? Where's the janitor? I've got that weird "alone" feeling again, even though there are people everywhere.

The noise around me escalates: clacking shoes on the floor, carnival organ music playing from a boom box, the hum of the cotton-candy maker, the whirr of the Wheel of Fortune, the chatter of teachers and students running back and forth. I see Val across the room, looking cool and collected, of course. She waves and grins confidently, as usual. I'm tempted to run over and scream "HELP!" but I don't. I just grin back. I have to figure this out for myself — fast.

I glance up at a clock on the wall. One o'clock on the dot. The doors to the room are about to fling open and here I am, missing three volunteers, standing like someone just yelled "FREEZE!" in a game of tag. I've gone from excited to panicked in no time. How will I fix this? Think, Taryn, think.

"Surf's up!" a voice bellows.

It's Principal Simms, standing over by the doors. I can't see if he's in swim trunks or not, but he appears to be wearing a blue plastic lei. My eyes scan the crowd of sixth, seventh, and eighth graders as they push into the room. One of the first people I see, heading right for my area of the carnival games, is Emma Wallace.

What else can possibly go wrong?!

I bury my face in my hands and hold my breath, trying to figure out what to do next.

That's when I hear his voice, coming closer.

It's Jeff.

Great, I think to myself. He's here with his crew: Jeff and the rest of the boys have come to the carnival to gloat, I just know it. They've come to see me fall flat on my face. After all, these are the dorks who called me Four Eyes last week.

"Taryn?"

I turn when Jeff calls my name. He's backed up by a cluster of guys from the soccer team. They're all wearing bright red soccer T-shirts.

"Jeff? Wh-wh-what are you doing here?" I stammer. My heart feels like it just stopped. I brace myself for the worst.

And then Jeff does the most incredible thing. He doesn't say anything mean or goofy. He doesn't say anything at all.

He just gives me one of his smiles.

That's when I know everything is going to be just fine.

Chapter 14

• • • JEFF • • •

No Sweat

When I see Taryn standing in front of that empty booth, I know I have to do something.

Sometimes friendships change, or at least that's what my mom keeps telling me. The other night she reminded me of this kid Chester Leonard who used to live up the block. Chester and I were inseparable for the entire summer after second grade. But then Chester decided to like another kid down the block. So he ditched me. Just like that. Right after he rode my bike over a nail and blew the tire.

That's what it felt like this week with Taryn. All week long, she has avoided me like the plague.

I saw her at lunch a few times. I saw her at her

locker once or twice. She hardly made eye contact. That was weird.

But I'm here now, trying to do something to fix it. I'm huddled outside the recreation room along with everyone else, waiting for the carnival to start. And five guys from soccer came along with me, including Jake.

Some teacher I don't know with a mustache is wearing a clown nose and holding a surfboard. He unlocks the door to the recreation room and welcomes everyone to the carnival. Principal Simms is standing there, too, in bright flowered shorts! Kids press into the room. Some run. Those are the kids looking for the big prizes. The air in here smells sticky sweet and my stomach does a flip-flop. I got super-sick one time at the circus when I ate three blue cotton candies and two snow cones in a row. I've never been the same.

There's beach art up on the wall and everything has some sort of title like SURF SEARCH or BEACH BOTTLE TOSS. It's a little lame, but fun at the same time. Half the teachers are running around in Hawaiian shirts. I can't help smiling.

The moment I enter the room, I spot Taryn standing by this ugly blow-up palm tree. She looks worried. Is she crying? Maybe she's thinking about our fight. Maybe she just misses me. I stride across the room with my new soccer buddies behind me, heading straight for Taryn and the tree.

When she sees me, she does a wild double take. But she doesn't move. It's like she's frozen in place or something.

"Jeff?" she says. "What are you doing here?" She still hasn't moved.

I smile.

"What's the deal? Nice carnival."

We both stand there, just staring, for another moment. All around us, kids rush to different games. The room is really loud with people chatting and music playing. Nearby, there are all these huge soda bottles lined up. Kids stand over them like giants with rings to toss, but there's no one to run the game.

"What's up with that?" I ask Taryn, pointing.

"It's one of the games I'm supposed to help organize," she says, her voice wavering like she's about to cry. "Only . . . no one . . . I don't . . ."

I step a little closer toward her and ask what's really wrong. I can tell when she's about to have one of her meltdowns.

"This is a total disaster," Taryn says, fighting back tears.

"Nah," I say. "It looks great. The room is packed."

"It's a disaster. I'm a disaster."

"What's up with your hair?"

"Hair?" Taryn grabs her head. "Oh. That," she says. "It's a new style."

"Yeah, I noticed." Even though she's about to lose it, Taryn looks good. I tell her, but she doesn't want to talk about it.

A moment later, Principal Simms walks over to us. He tugs on his blue lei and I can read his T-shirt: ALOHA MAN.

I'm tempted to crack up. But Taryn looks like she's about to puke.

"Hello, Miss Taylor," the Principal says in a deep voice.

How does he know her name? That's amazing. Then I realize she's wearing a name tag.

Duh.

"I just want to thank you for your help," the Principal says, shaking Taryn's hand.

She nods politely but I can tell that under the surface, Taryn is majorly unsteady. Her face gets all pink and speckled like it does when she's about to freak out.

As soon as Principal Simms walks away, Taryn sighs and turns to me.

"I'm glad you're here," she confesses.

"I know," I say. "Maybe we could help you out."

"Help? *Me?*"

I nod. "Sure. Who else would I help?"

I'm thrown off balance completely when, all at once, Taryn flings her arms around me and squeezes me like I'm a gigantic lemon. She's never done that before. I quickly look back at the guys. No one's really paying any attention, thankfully.

"Uh . . . Taryn, you can let go now," I plead, pushing her away. Unfortunately, her earring is caught on my shirt. For a split second, we're stuck together.

"Sorry," she says, removing the earring as we pull apart.

"So, do you need any help from us or what?" I ask.

"YES! I do!"

Taryn bursts into giggles. She does that a lot. In between laughs, she shows me and the other soccer guys over to the games and activities that need people to run them. She's all business now, the take-charge Taryn that I've known forever. I grab a trio of large rings and pass them off to the first kid in line.

I can do this. No sweat.

Before I know it, Taryn has put us all to work and things are in full swing. The games are drawing a huge crowd.

But actually, working the carnival is more fun than I expected. I could do it all day. Luckily, after a while the trio of *real* volunteers from Taryn's team shows up to do their jobs, so we stand-ins don't have to run the game for very long. They give Taryn some lame excuse about getting the times mixed up. I expect her to read them the riot act, but instead she thanks them for coming at all. Wow. She really does deal under pressure.

As we're standing there, Mr. Wood comes over and pats Taryn on the back.

"You have to be one of the most organized carnival leaders I've ever had," he says. "You had a team of volunteers — and then you had backup helpers, too. Very fine, very fine. I certainly hope you'll be a carnival leader next year, too."

Part of me wants to laugh out loud and say, "Are you kidding me? You should have seen her about a half hour ago! She was a MESS!"

But of course I say nothing. When it comes to Taryn, I'm learning that sometimes I need to just keep my trap shut.

After being relieved of our ring toss duties, a couple of the soccer guys and I decide to play some games. I win three in a row at the bean-bag toss and snag a princess bear (or at least that's what it looks like, with its cheesy pink plastic crown). Blair will love it. Maybe if she plays with it, she'll leave Toots alone. I can only hope.

At some point, Jake and I hit the jackpot at the Wheel of Fortune, spinning the wheel to reveal a truly grand prize: a supersized Hershey's bar. He's allergic to chocolate, so he gives me the whole thing. I down the bar in only three bites, hardly any chews: a new personal record.

Eventually, Peter and Anthony show up and find me and the rest of the gang, too. Eight of us pose together in a fake beach photo booth where we stand there holding beat-up surfboards and wearing plastic leis. I ham it up, as usual. Some girls standing off to the side make "hoo-hoo" noises. That cracks me up. Then I realize *who* is making all the noise.

It's TLC: Taryn, Leslie, and Cristina.

Humiliation city.

There's one side effect from the whole carnival experience that I didn't even consider. I found five very cool guys on the team to be my friends. We're only a couple of weeks into sixth grade, but I feel like I've been here way longer, and it's all worth it.

It's all good.

Chapter 15

✿ ✿ ✿ TARYN ✿ ✿ ✿

Until the Butterflies Come Back

The air smells like wet leaves because it's raining this morning. I love rainy Saturdays, especially after a long week, and this week was the longest week in the history of weeks. But even though it was tough, I rediscovered all the reasons why Jeff is my best guy friend. He saved me, plain and simple. I guess that means I owe him — big time — and he'll probably collect. But that's okay. The carnival would not have been a success without him.

I stand up from our sofa and stretch. Zsa-Zsa stretches, too. She loves the rain as long as she's inside the house, safe and dry, buried deep into someone's lap or a cushiony chair.

Fall is really here now. I can practically taste it.

Freshly picked apples, pumpkins, and Indian corn are showing up at the supermarket. Tim, Tom, and Todd said something about the four of us hopping in the car this week to go apple-picking up at Brown Farms. We go every year. Last year, we carted home four bushels of apples. Mom made bread, cookies, pies, tarts, and more. In fact, that was when she really got into the whole cooking thing. I blame the apples.

Gazing out of our big bay window, I can see Jeff's porch from our living room. He said he'd come out to see me soon. The moment he appears through his screen door, I hop right out of my seat, grab my slicker, and head outside to join him.

Zsa-Zsa mews loudly as I leave, but she has no intention of following me.

As I step out, I can feel that it's spitting again; not steady rain, but wet nonetheless.

"Hey, T!" Jeff calls out to me.

I race over to his porch, sidestepping puddles on our sidewalk. I can't cut through the bushes today because they're too wet.

"Hey," I gasp, collapsing into one of the wicker rockers. I peel off my jacket. It's too warm to keep it on.

"Can you even see through those things?" Jeff asks, pointing at my glasses.

I take off my glasses to wipe away the raindrops. It's hard getting used to glasses and weather. When it's too hot and I walk into an air-conditioned room, my glasses steam up. When it rains, they get wet, like now.

"You know, they look good," Jeff blurts.

"What?"

"Your glasses. They look good."

"Oh. Thanks," I reply. *Huh.*

"They make you look older," Jeff says.

We sit there, rocking back and forth for a while without saying anything very important. It's been weeks — since just before school started — since we did this together.

I miss Jeff so much, but things feel different now. *Way* different.

"You're wearing your hair down again, huh?" Jeff says.

"Do you like it?" I ask Jeff, tugging at the ends. "It's a little frizzy today with the rain."

Jeff nods. "It's cool. But I like it when you wear a ponytail, too."

When he says that, something inside my belly twists, like butterflies, only I can't quite explain why. Normally, Jeff would make fun of any hairdo long before he'd compliment it. So why is he doing the opposite today?

155

"Thanks," I say, not knowing how else to respond.

"Yeah, well . . ." Jeff's voice drifts off. He kicks at the bottom of his chair, nearly bonking poor Toots. When the dog lets out a little howl, Jeff reaches down to make sure Toots is okay.

"Hey, did I tell you that I got a new video game?" Jeff asks, completely changing the subject.

"Not Killer Robots!" I squeal. I've been dying to play that game ever since I heard it had come out.

Jeff chuckles. "Yeah, it's Killer Robots. It looks hard, but I haven't really checked out all the levels. You want to play?"

I smile. "Of course I do," I say. I'm wondering if now that I have glasses, maybe I'll be able to beat him at video games. Usually I'm ten thousand points behind.

"I'm warning you," Jeff says, smiling. "I've been practicing a little bit."

I know he's been at it for days. He's always faking me out when it comes to playing games.

"So let's go," he says. "J.D. just hooked up a new TV in the basement."

As we stand up to go inside, I stumble over a loose board on the porch. My sandal flips off and I go falling right into Jeff's arms. This pushes him backward, unsteady. We end up in a big pile right at the edge of his porch steps.

Toots lets out an even louder howl.

"Ouch!" I squeal. But I'm the one squashing him.

"Your superstrength is no match for me, Wonder Woman." Jeff laughs, trying to push me up.

"Watch it, Aquaman!" I laugh back.

We try to stand at the same time, but it's no use. We can't seem to untangle. Rain spills down from the gutters, spraying us like a fountain.

Finally, Jeff gets free, stands up, sticks out his damp hand, and helps me to my feet. It takes me a while to steady myself. For whatever reason, Jeff doesn't let go of my hand right away.

As he's holding my fingers in his, I feel all fluttery again. Thoughts flood into my head. I think of all those things L and C said to me over the summer. I think of how Jeff came to help me at the carnival. I follow him inside, feeling safe — and close.

Wait.

This isn't a crush, I tell myself. Leslie and Cristina don't know what they're talking about. I can't crush on someone I've known since we were in diapers.

No way.

Jeff is my friend. F-R-I-E-N-D. I don't like boys

that way. Besides, all that matters at this exact moment is getting hooked up to Jeff's brand-new video game and destroying every last one of his killer robots.

That's my plan. And I'm sticking to it.

Until, of course, the butterflies come back again.

About the Author

Laura Dower has never fake-swallowed a worm (like Jeff) or been a carnival leader (like Taryn), but she did have a longtime crush on a boy who lived next door. She's the author of more than 70 books for kids, including the series From the Files of Madison Finn. She lives in New York with her husband, two kids, and laptop computer. Check out her Web site: www.lauradower.com.

check out

THE
Accidental
CHEERLEADER

Another
candy apple book . . .
just for you.

candy
apple

Sophie leaned against her locker and checked her watch for the third time that morning. Eight-fifteen. The hall was starting to fill with students. Noise echoed through the corridor as they hollered greetings, excited to see one another after the summer. A few kids Sophie knew said hi as they passed her and her best friend, Kylie. They all were wearing bright clothes in the latest fashions. They sported new haircuts and dark tans, and the ones who'd gotten their braces off flashed extra-wide pearly white smiles.

The first day of the school year wasn't really like school at all, Sophie thought. It was more like a commercial for school. All the kids wore cool clothes and looked happy, the teachers acted nice, and the classes actually seemed interesting. It was like watching a movie preview that turns out to be way better than the movie itself.

Just then, there was a ripple in the flow of hallway movement. Several kids turned to look as a quartet of girls strode down the center of the corridor.

In the lead was a petite girl with almond-shaped eyes and long wavy black hair that reached halfway down her back. Everyone in school knew Keisha Reyes. She was head of the cheerleading team and the most popular girl at Meridian. The red-haired girl to her right, walking so close that she matched Keisha's steps, was her best friend, Courtney Knox. Following on their heels were two blonde girls — Amie and Marie Gildencrest, the only identical twins at Meridian Middle School. Courtney, Amie, and Marie were all cheerleaders, too.

As they walked down the hall, the girls shouted greetings to the other popular eighth-graders. Keisha had a perfect smile, Sophie noticed. It was wide and full of even, white teeth. Courtney, on the other hand, looked like she was pouting even when she wasn't. Sophie thought it was because of all the lip gloss she wore.

"Heeeey, Scott!" Keisha called flirtatiously as she passed.

Scott flashed his crooked grin and waved at her.

Someone called Sophie's and Kylie's names. A

boy's voice. Confused, Sophie pulled her gaze from the cheerleaders and looked around. There was Joel Leo making his way toward them through the crowded hallway.

Joel had moved in down the street from Kylie the year before, at the beginning of sixth grade. They had become friends riding the bus together. Sophie had gotten to know him a little, too, when she took the bus home with Kylie after school.

"Joel-e-o!" Kylie exclaimed.

"Hey, Joel," said Sophie.

"What's up, guys?" he said. "How was your summer?"

"Oh, you know, the usual," Kylie answered, with a bored wave of her hand. "Jetting to Hollywood. Shopping in London. Sunbathing in Saint Trapeze."

Joel smiled. "You mean Saint-Tropez?"

"Yeah, there, too," Kylie said.

Joel and Sophie laughed. "We mostly hung out at the pool," Sophie told him. "What about you?"

"Yeah, I didn't see you around," Kylie added.

"I was in California helping out on my aunt and uncle's farm," Joel told them. "They grow organic kiwis. Weird, huh?"

"Weird," Sophie agreed. "But it sounds kind of cool, too."

"It was pretty cool. They paid me six dollars an hour to pick fruit, and I got to eat all the kiwis I wanted. I don't really like them, though. Kiwis, I mean. They're all furry."

"Gross!" Kylie said. "So you spent the summer eating furry fruit? Sounds like a blast."

Joel smiled. "Naw, most of my family lives around there, too. I have some cousins who are pretty cool. They taught me how to surf."

The way he said "surf" gave Sophie a little chill. She tried to imagine Joel eating tropical fruit and surfing in southern California. It seemed incredibly exotic compared to hanging out by the pool. Sophie always found Joel slightly mysterious. He didn't look like most of the other boys at Meridian. His hair was long and a little shaggy, and he wore T-shirts for bands that Sophie had never heard of. Even his name was unusual. Joel Leo. If you took off the *J* it was the same spelled forward and backward.

What impressed Sophie most, though, was how laid-back Joel seemed. She couldn't imagine starting middle school in a new town where you didn't know anyone, but Joel didn't seem to mind at all. In sixth grade, he'd been just as friendly with the math nerds as he was with the skaters and the soccer players. As far as Sophie could tell, he wasn't part of any clique. He got along with a lot of different kids.

Sophie noticed how his teeth stood out white against his brown face. *He got tan over the summer,* she thought. *He looks good. In fact, he's cute. Way cute.*

As quickly as the thought came, Sophie pushed it away. Kylie and Joel were neighbors, and their parents were friends. She knew their families sometimes had dinner together, which in Sophie's mind practically made them related. If Kylie found out she had a crush on Joel, she'd never hear the end of it.

The bell for first period rang loudly, startling Sophie out of her thoughts.

"Well, I better go," Joel said. "I'll see you guys later." His eyes rested on Sophie for a moment. She felt the beginnings of a blush creep into her cheeks.

"Later, Joeleo," Kylie said cheerfully.

"Bye," Sophie murmured.

"Hey, by the way, Kylie," Joel said as he walked away, "cool pants!"

Kylie beamed. Sophie gritted her teeth, hating her lime green cords.

Later that day, Sophie stretched her legs across the seat in the last row of the bus. She worked the flavor out of a piece of cinnamon gum.

Kylie was sprawled out on the seat in front of

Sophie, and Joel lounged in the seat across the aisle. Sophie was going over to Kylie's as she usually did after school, and both Kylie's and Joel's houses were the last stop on the bus route. The bus was mostly empty now, so they had taken over the back rows of seats.

"I heard Keisha was dating a high-school guy over the summer," Kylie reported.

Kylie had spent the last fifteen minutes reviewing the summer gossip she'd picked up at school. Most of it centered around Keisha Reyes.

"I heard she dumped him right before school started," Kylie went on. "And he spent every night for a week calling her on the phone, crying and begging her to get back together. Can you imagine? A high-school guy!"

"What grade in high-school?" Joel asked.

"I'm not sure. Ninth, I think."

"Big deal. If he's in ninth grade that means he was in eighth grade last year. Which means he's practically the same age as Keisha," Joel pointed out.

Kylie shrugged defensively. "It's just what I heard."

"Anyway, I'm tired of hearing about Keisha Reyes. She's a snob," said Joel.

"Maybe people just *think* she's a snob because she's a cheerleader and she's pretty and popular. Maybe she's actually really nice. She has nice hair," Kylie pointed out.

"That's great logic, Kylie," Joel said. "Just because someone has nice hair doesn't mean she's a nice person."

Sophie sighed and let her attention drift. She wondered what it would be like to have a guy beg you to get back together. The crying part sounded awful, she decided. But it still would be nice to have a guy like you so much he called every night.

Sophie had never had a boyfriend. Not a real one, anyway. In fourth grade a boy named Tyler had asked her to go out with him, but they didn't go anywhere and it didn't really mean anything. But she knew having a boyfriend was different in middle school. Girls held their boyfriends' hands. They hung out by their lockers and went to the movies. They even kissed.

She glanced across the aisle at Joel. He was wearing a black T-shirt that said THE RAMONES in bold white letters. A loop of his long light brown hair fell against his cheek. He tucked it behind his ear. Unconsciously, Sophie brought her hand to her face and tucked her own hair behind her ear.

Joel felt her gaze and looked over. When he met Sophie's eyes, he smiled. Quickly, Sophie turned her attention back to Kylie.

"Anyway," Kylie was saying, "I guess we'll know what they're all like pretty soon. We're probably going to be spending a lot of time with them."

"Spending a lot of time with whom?" Sophie asked. "What are you talking about?"

"Keisha and the other cheerleaders," Kylie told her. "Tryouts for the team are next week. I think we have a shot at making it."

"You're trying out for cheerleading?" Sophie was surprised. Kylie hadn't mentioned it before.

Kylie's smile could have lit up a football stadium. "Nope. *We're* trying out. I signed you up, too!"

There was a squeal of brakes as the bus lurched to a halt at Joel and Kylie's stop. Sophie sat bolt upright and stared over the seat back at her friend. "You did *what*?"